Matt
The Moody
Hermit Crab

Matt
The Moody
Hermit Crab

Love & blessings,

Caroline C. McGee

Caroline C. McGee

McGee & Woods
Nashville

Published by

McGee & Woods, Inc.
631 Second Avenue South, Suite 1R
Nashville, Tennessee 37210

Printed and bound in the United States of America

This is a work of fiction. Names, characters, places, and
incidents are either the product of the author's imagination
or are used fictitiously. Any resemblance to actual events
or locales or persons, living or dead, is entirely coinciden-
tal.

ISBN 1-891347-05-5 (hardcover)

FIRST PRINTING
10 9 8 7 6 5 4 3 2 1

*To Joel and all those who share this
difficult journey and*

*To Connie who helped pave the way to
a brighter tomorrow*

Contents

CHAPTER 1
Call Me "Unpredictable"

"Ow," Abby cried. "You pinched me. I'm gonna tell Mom!" Abby scurried down the hallway noisily bumping against the wall a couple of times with her large purple crab claw. Matt was following close behind her as his dark red legs moved quickly in pursuit.

"Mommm," Abby wailed. "Matt pinched me again. I didn't do anything to him. He is so mean." Abby and Matt raced to the blue couch where their mom was reading.

"Now settle down you two," Ali replied calmly.

Matt caught up with Abby and roughly pushed her aside. The bumping of their shells made a loud clanking sound. Abby held her ground and pushed back.

"Abby, just stay away from him when he's in one of his moods," Ali warned as her eyes peered up just in time to see the two wrestling.

"She started it," Matt accused. "She is so nosey. And she

never stops talking. She makes me so angry sometimes." Matt waved his claws in the air and stamped the wood floor with his legs.

"That's right. You're always angry or acting stupid," Abby said with a sneer and turned the back of her white spiral shell toward him.

"Oh, shut up, dummy," Matt replied and turned toward his room. His brown and white swirled shell slammed hard against the wall knocking plaster loose. Pieces of plaster drifted to the floor. The light brown wall had many small holes and marks from Matt's frequent spells of anger and frustration.

"Nobody understands me, and nobody cares. I just wish I was dead." Matt hurried to his room and slammed the door with a loud thud.

Ali took a deep breath, set her book aside and followed him down the hallway. Her green, white and yellow shell was a large impressive spiral. Her long purplish red legs were strong and tapered to fine white tips, but she moved gracefully and quietly. She knocked gently on his bedroom's black wooden door with her large purple claw. Matt had painted the door just a few weeks ago. He claimed that he wanted the door's color to match his feelings.

"Matt, please tell me what's wrong. Why are you so angry?" she asked.

"It's nothin', Mom. Just go away. I don't feel like talking about it," Matt replied. His voice sounded sad and lonely.

"Honey, I just want to help you. Is there a problem at school? Is it your friends? What's going on?" Ali asked in a worried tone of voice and tilted her head up to the door to listen. Only silence greeted her. She turned back to Abby who had come along behind her. Ali sighed and the two started back down the hallway passing Abby's room on the way. Her room's walls were painted pink, and she had drawn flowers and butterflies on them. She had a small bed with pictures of little mermaids on the cover and a little vanity with a lighted mirror.

"I told you he's a jerk. He's so mean, and he says mean things to me all the time," Abby blurted out.

"What does Matt say to you?" Ali asked stopping to look at her.

"Well, like that I'm dumb as dirt or ugly as a fish's behind," Abby replied. "He tells me he wishes he didn't have to live with anybody as dumb or ugly as me. He hurts my feelings. Why is he so mean, Mom? Why?" Abby started to cry. Ali placed a comforting claw around her and drew her close.

"Abby, you'll be fine. And you know that those things aren't true. You are neither dumb nor ugly," her mother reassured. "I just hope Matt snaps out of this nasty mood he's in real soon," she added. Ali and Abby settled down on the couch.

"What's on TV?" Abby asked. But before Ali could even answer her question, they were startled by Ben's voice.

"Mommm," Ben's voice rumbled down the hallway. "Matt is acting weird again. You'd better come quick!" Ben opened the door to reveal Matt laughing so hard he couldn't get up off the floor. He was rocking back and forth on the back of his shell giggling and then laughing loudly about a joke only he seemed to know. Ali and Abby rushed back up the hallway.

"What's going on now?" Ali asked.

"I don't know," replied Ben with his claws raised up over

his head. "Matt said something about hearing a funny joke today at school and started laughing. I can't get him to stop." Ben was the oldest. His hand-painted shell was swirled with orange, yellow, green, blue, and purple. Normally he was calm and liked being in control, but now he looked confused and frightened. "Mom, he's acting so weird. He really scares me."

"Matt, Matt, tell me what's going on?" Ali repeated. "Five or ten minutes ago you were so angry, and now you're laughing like you're out of your mind."

He ignored her and continued to laugh uncontrollably until Ali finally yelled, "Matt, stop it! Stop it right now!"

Immediately Matt stopped laughing. He looked startled and confused. He was lying in the middle of Ben's floor on his back. And then he started to cry. "You don't love me. Nobody loves me. You're just a mean mom, and I don't love you either. I wish you were dead! I wish all of you were dead!" He stood up and stomped out of Ben's room. Once inside his room, Matt pulled into his shell and refused to come out. None of Ali's begging or pleading was able to coax him out of his shell.

Ali slowly rolled her eyes and shook her antennae. She looked tired as though she had been in a battle all night. She felt like it too. "All right gang, it's getting late and you need to get ready for bed. You have school in the morning." She prodded Ben and Abby toward their rooms. "We'll talk about this in the morning. I'm too tired and confused to try and figure out what's going on with Matt right now." "But I wanted to watch TV," Abby protested.

"Not now, Abby," Ali replied sternly. "It's time to go to bed." She made sure that each of them got a good-night kiss except for Matt. She could only kiss the outside of his shell.

"I love you, Matt. I hope you feel better in the morning," Ali whispered gently. She was hoping he might whisper back, but he didn't. A tear slid down the outside of his shell and made a tiny puddle on the floor. Her heart ached. She loved Matt, but he seemed to be slipping away from her.

Ali went to bed, but she couldn't sleep because she was so worried about Matt. She thought about how strange he had been acting lately. She wondered why his behavior had changed so much. After several hours, she fell asleep hoping he would be better in the morning.

CHAPTER 2
Schoolyard Trouble

The early morning sun was just starting to reflect off the ocean waves lapping lazily outside the front door. Curious rays of sunlight gently danced through Ali's bedroom window and sparkled upon Abby's shell. The white lace curtains swayed in the morning breeze. Still very sleepy, Ali struggled to listen to Abby's urgent complaint.

"Mom, Mom, wake up," Abby cried. "Matt is tearing up one of Ben's favorite books." Ali could hear Ben shouting at Matt and begging him not to do it. She roused herself up and hurried down the hallway weaving slightly from side to side to where the boys were arguing.

Ben's room was at the end of the hall and resembled a planetarium. He had models of Saturn V rockets and the Space Shuttle on his shelves. Each of the nine planets had been lovingly hand-painted and hung from the ceiling with thin string. A large poster of the Sun, complete with red and yellow flaming solar flares leaping from the surface of the computer-generated image, hung on one wall.

"Please, Matt. Please don't tear it up. You know how much I love that book," Ben begged. "That's my book about space and rockets, and please don't tear it up."

"Bet you won't mess with me again, will you Benny boy?" Matt replied. His eyes were wild and glassy. He didn't look like Matt anymore. He danced around gleefully and laughed a mean and scary kind of laugh. "Watch me destroy your favorite book one page at a time," Matt said as he began to rip out the first page.

"Stop it! Stop it right this minute, Matt!" Ali shouted and grabbed the book away from him. "How dare you do this? Your father will be so angry with you. I'll let him punish you when he gets home tonight. I am so disappointed in you." The angry quiver and force in Ali's voice frightened Matt and he jumped back away from her.

"Are you going to hurt me?" Matt asked shaking and acting like he was scared. "You are so mean. You're just a big bully picking on me. Why did you yell at me?"

"What are you talking about?" Ali asked. "You were dancing around here like a devil tearing up your brother's favorite book and you tell me that I'm a bully!" Ali took a slow, deep breath and calmed herself down. "Matt, you have been acting so strangely lately. We don't know what to think."

"I don't know what you're talkin' about," Matt replied quickly. "It's just your imagination, Mom. Hey, don't we need to get ready for school?" Matt hurried toward his room and closed the door.

Ali stood in shocked silence for a moment. Her claw was over her open mouth and then she asked, "Ben, what just happened?"

"I don't know, Mom. What do you mean?" Ben asked cocking his antennae to one side.

"Matt! What just happened with Matt? He was terrorizing you and destroying your book. I stopped him, and suddenly I'm a mean bully. And then it's like nothing ever happened. Am I the one going insane here?" Ali's voice grew shrill.

"No, Mom, it's not you, it's Matt. He's the one who acts like he came from another planet," Ben replied.

"He's a jerk, Mom. Do you think maybe he got abducted by aliens?" Abby proposed with a giggle.

"Maybe, maybe not, but either way, you two do need to get ready for school. Go get some breakfast and get your books. I think I'll walk with you to school today," Ali said and headed for the bathroom to clean up. "Matt, I'll meet you at the back door in a few minutes," she called as she passed his door.

Suddenly Matt's door opened and he jumped out into the hallway. "Why are you going with us, Mom? You haven't walked us to school for at least two years now," Matt asked suspiciously.

"I need to go to school anyway, so I thought I'd walk with you," she answered.

Ben and Abby dutifully waited in the back yard for their mother. Ben dribbled his basketball and dodged imaginary opponents while Abby drew pictures of flowers in the sand. Their house faced the ocean nestled in a modest neighborhood of three and four bedroom houses. Their school was close enough to walk, so Ali insisted they do so whenever the weather was nice.

As Ben and Abby waited, Matt hurried ahead.

"You'd better wait for Mom," Abby called.

"I'm not waitin' for nobody," Matt yelled back as he raced ahead.

"You will if you know what's good for you," Ben called.

"Mom's gonna be mad," Abby yelled.

"Who cares?" Matt called back.

"You will when your father gets home," was the reply that made him stop. Ben, Abby, and Ali caught up with Matt, who looked worried and was unusually quiet. When they arrived at school, Ali found Matt's teacher Ms. Kay.

Ms. Kay, a sea gull, was at her desk preparing for the day's lessons. She was perched on a stool in front of her easel-shaped desk. Her glasses were atop her light yellow beak as she gazed down at her papers. Her feathers were soft gray along her back and wings and white everywhere else except for her tail. Her tail feathers were jet black. Her pink feet were propped up on the rungs of the stool on which she was sitting.

"Ms. Kay?" Ali cleared her throat. "May I have a moment of your time?" she asked.

Ms. Kay peered over her glasses and motioned with her wing for her to come in. "Good morning. How are you today?" she asked.

"I'm Ali Lavar, Matt's mom," she said.

"Oh yes, we met at the open house a couple of months ago. It's nice to see you again," Ms. Kay replied extending her wing to Ali.

"I was wondering if you have noticed any problems with Matt's behavior." Ali asked.

Ms. Kay adjusted her glasses with her right wing and looked like she was thinking. "What kind of behavior?" she asked and then decided to answer her own question. "Matt is an active little crab, and he gets into a fair amount of trouble, but I haven't seen anything that would make me ask him to leave my classroom."

"Well, that's good to hear," Ali replied. "We've been having some problems with him at home, and I wondered if they were showing up at school. I guess not."

Ali turned to go. "Thank you for your time, Ms. Kay. Please let me know if Matt does cause any problems," she added. Ali returned home quietly thinking about Matt, Abby, and Ben. She considered what she would tell their father when he came home that night. She felt very tired and empty. It would be good to have another adult in the house. Ali listened to the soothing ebb and flow of the ocean waves as she walked. She gazed at the houses in the neighborhood. It appeared there were two new ones being built. She saw the younger crabs playing with their mothers on the beach and remembered when Abby and Matt were still at home during the day. Ben had just started school. She would walk with Ben on the little sandy path behind the houses with Abby and Matt in a stroller. Life seemed easier back then. "We were happier," she thought.

At school that day Ms. Kay tried to ignore Matt's behavior, but he could not be still or stay out of arguments. She was giving a spelling test to the class, but Matt couldn't stay in his seat.

"Matt, please stay seated until the test is finished," Ms. Kay directed.

"I can't," Matt replied acting very nervously. "I have to go outside."

"Why do you have to go outside, Matt?" she asked.

"Because everybody is looking at me," Matt replied. He stood up and started to walk to the outside door of the classroom.

"Matt, you cannot leave the room," Ms. Kay told him.

"I have to," he replied. "I'll die if I stay in here. They will kill me. They all want to kill me. I have to get away." Matt hurried out the door leaving Ms. Kay speechless. She stood in the middle of the room with her beak open, but no words came out. This was a rare event. Ms. Kay usually had a wise and witty comment for nearly every situation, but not this time. She was stumped.

"Stop, Matt, you can't go out," Ms. Kay called. By now the entire class was aware that something was going on. Whispers began breaking out and girls began to giggle. She glanced around to find the fastest crab in her room. "Carl," she called. "Please tell Matt to come in or he will have to go to the principal's office."

"Yes, Ma'am," Carl replied.

So Carl rushed dutifully out the door and delivered the message to Matt. Carl was a white ghost crab and could run very fast.

Ms. Kay turned back to her class. "Please turn in your test and start reading chapter five in your science book," she said. "Everything is going to be fine."

Carl returned in a few moments without Matt. "Matt refuses to come, Ms. Kay," Carl spoke in quick short spurts. He was breathing hard. Carl's black eyes stood out on long stalks and darted back and forth rapidly. "He's hiding in an old tire out near the playground. I can't get him to budge. He acts like he's scared to death."

Ms. Kay was growing more concerned. She needed to get Matt back inside the classroom, but the normal warnings and reasoning were not working. Then she had an unusual idea.

"Carl, please go back out and tell Matt that he needs to come in before he catches a cold," Ms. Kay requested. The room filled with laughter at Ms. Kay's proposal. The whispers grew louder and names could be heard.

Carl appeared puzzled; his eyes darted back and forth and stopped, and he replied, "But Ms. Kay, it isn't cold outside."

Another round of laughter rippled through the classroom.

"That's okay, Carl, just tell Matt anyway," Ms. Kay answered.

Carl hurried outside to tell Matt. Ms. Kay whirled around to face her class. "That's enough! I am disappointed that you are not doing what I asked. Instead you have been eavesdropping on my conversation with Carl. So I guess you need more work," Ms. Kay threatened sternly. Disapproving groans filled the air. "Then I advise you to be thoughtful of others who are having problems and not make fun of them unless you want extra work," she added.

"Yes, Ma'am," was the collective reply.

Carl returned and this time with Matt by his side. Matt sat quietly in his seat. Ms. Kay decided not to say anything to him about his odd behavior.

By lunchtime Matt seemed okay and was joking with his friends. While munching on fruit and bread, Joey, Billy, Matt, and Todd were trying to tell the grossest jokes they could think of.

Joey, the biggest of the boys, was a Florida snapping turtle. He had a large head and powerful jaws. His dark eyes were set on the side of his head in shallow sockets. He had a large brownish-black oval shell with thick and scaly, rough brown webbed legs for swimming and sharp claws on his feet for climbing. Joey's tail was the same color and texture as his legs. Even though he was bigger, Joey was friendly, gentle and loved to talk. Todd, a stone crab, was much smaller but stout with a brownish-red shell covered with lots of gray spots. The tips of his claws were black and his legs were short and strong. Todd tended to be a little on the quiet side. Billy was a red rock lobster. His legs were short, but his body was long with a fan-like tail. He had two large and uneven pincer claws. Along with short eyestalks and round black eyes, he also had two long red antennae that looked almost like whiskers. Billy giggled a lot.

"Matt that is the stupidest thing I have ever heard. You have got to be crazy," Joey said loudly. Billy and Todd laughed and nodded. He slapped Matt's shell in a friendly manner. It jarred Matt and startled him.

Matt suddenly became angry. He looked around trying to find something to throw at the laughing trio.

"Don't laugh at me," Matt cried. "I'm not stupid, you are." He found a large rock a few inches away and quickly lifted it over his head and threw it in their direction. It fell with a loud thud directly in front of them. Suddenly they stopped laughing. They backed away quickly.

"Now I know you're crazy, Matt," Joey called over his back as he hurried toward the classroom.

Ms. Kay saw the whole incident. She thought to herself, "Something is seriously wrong with Matt. Surely he is too young to be abusing drugs or alcohol. His behavior is so frightening and it changes so quickly from one extreme to the other. He can be so sweet and then in the blink of an eye, he can be very angry, tearful or terrified. How am I supposed to handle a student like him?"

Matt ran to hide from his friends for fear they might come back and hurt him. He stood with his face against the wall of the school building in a dark corner. Ms. Kay found him. "Matt, are you all right?" Ms. Kay asked.

Matt recognized her voice and didn't turn around. "Why are they so mean to me? I didn't do anything to them," Matt sobbed.

"Actually, Matt, you threw a large rock at them which I

consider *doing something* to your friends. And the conversation I overheard should not have made you angry," Ms. Kay replied.

"But he hit me, Ms. Kay. Joey hit me on the shell," Matt cried and pointed to the spot where his friend had jokingly slapped him.

"Matt, please turn around and look at me," Ms. Kay requested.

Matt slowly turned around to face Ms. Kay. She peered into his eyes and said, "Joey wasn't trying to hurt you. He was just showing you that he accepted you. He thought you were funny."

A look of horror came over Matt's face as he realized that he had misunderstood Joey's actions. "I've messed up again," Matt sobbed dropping his face into his claws.

Now Ms. Kay was confused. She thought that this news would make Matt feel better, but it made him feel even worse.

"I think I need to take you to the clinic, and give you a chance to calm down. This has been a hard day for you and a little quiet time away from the class will probably help you," Ms. Kay replied and gently ushered Matt toward the clinic area.

Matt spent the rest of the day in the clinic, and Ms. Kay returned to the classroom. The clinic had three cots for students who weren't feeling well or had been hurt on the playground. Matt sat on a cot staring at the walls. The cinderblock walls were painted gray and a clock was mounted on one of them. There was a poster about healthy eating habits and one about good oral hygiene. Students' moms volunteered to cover shifts each day in the clinic. Matt's mom was on the schedule to cover one day next month. Julie's mom was working today. Matt didn't feel like talking to her.

CHAPTER 3
Two Bad Moods Don't Make a Right

When school was out at 3:30 PM, Matt was still in a bad mood walking home with Abby and Ben.

"How was your day, Abby?" Ben asked. "Are you doing your times tables yet?"

Abby loved to sing and talk and seemed to enjoy hearing herself do both. "It was lovely, Ben, and yes, I'm learning the times tables, but I need some help with my math homework. Could you help me with it when we get home?" she asked.

"How about you, Matt? Hear any good jokes today?" Ben asked kindly.

"Oh, shut up. You two make me want to throw up," Matt replied angrily. "And how are you, Ben? And how are you, Abby?" he squeaked out making fun of Ben's and Abby's pleasant conversation.

"That's enough!" Ben shouted. "You are so selfish. You don't care about anybody but yourself." The anger in Ben's voice startled Matt, and he hurried off ahead of them in silence.

"I don't know how much more of him I can stand," Ben murmured to Abby. She nodded in agreement.

"You're right, Ben. Matt really is a jerk. He's a mean, selfish, ugly jerk. I don't know why we have to live with him. Why don't Mom and Dad send him away somewhere?" Abby asked placing her small claw up to her face.

The two continued toward home. "Abby, Mom and Dad can't just send Matt away. They love him as much as they love us. It's just not that simple," Ben replied as they headed in the back door.

Their dad had returned from his business trip by dinnertime. Hampton was his real name, but everyone called him Ham. He was an Ecuadorian hermit crab. His eyes were dark rectangles on short stalks. He had short hairy growths like a mustache. His legs were tan with bluish tips and both his claws were a brownish color. Ham's shell was a large spiral shape with an orange-salmon color mixed with white and purple. The tip of the spiral was on the right side and it stuck out a couple of inches further than it did on the left. To get close enough to whisper to Ham, you had to stand on his left.

"Time for dinner," Ali called. "Wash up before you come." Matt was going into the bathroom as Abby was leaving. They collided in the doorway.

"What is your problem, stupid?" Matt yelled at Abby.

"Who are you calling stupid?" Abby yelled back. "You are the one who knocked me down."

"You're just a klutzy whatsy," Matt replied mockingly.

"I am not, dodo brain," Abby cried. "Mommm, Matt's doing it again."

Ali jumped up from the table and hurried to break up the fight. Ham was still sitting at the table.

"When are we going to eat?" Ham called. "I've been gone for three days and you'd think somebody would be glad I'm home."

Ali pinned Matt to the wall to shield Abby. "Abby, run on to the table and serve your father. I'll take care of Matt," she said. Abby nodded and hurried to the dinner table. "Ben, where are you?" Ali called.

Ben came out of his room with his small stereo headphones still dangling from his shell. "What, Mom? I'm sorry I was doing my homework and couldn't hear you," Ben replied. Ali looked half amused and said, "I'm sure you couldn't hear me with those headphones on your shell."

Ben glanced down and saw the cord and realized he had been caught. "I, uh, I'm sorry, Mom. I was listening to my music. Can I help you with dinner?" Ben asked sheepishly.

"Go help your sister serve dinner, please," Ali replied with a sly and weary grin. Ben hurried to do as she asked.

"As for you, Matt, I'm going to tell your father how out of control you've become. That little book-destroying party won't go over too well, I'm sure," Ali warned.

"Go ahead and tell him. I don't care," Matt bluffed. "He won't believe you anyway. I can be a little angel if I want to," he replied with an evil grin.

"Let's go, buster," she demanded and marched him to the table.

Ham had already started eating and seemed annoyed that dinner had been delayed. "What's the problem? I thought we were supposed to be eating dinner," he remarked.

"Matt has been a little difficult to deal with lately," Ali replied. She motioned for Matt to sit down. He did so grudgingly.

"So what's the problem, Matt? Why are you giving your mother such a hard time?" Ham asked.

Matt shoveled food into his mouth quickly and lifted both of his claws up to his head like he didn't know the answer. Everyone waited for an answer to Dad's question, but Matt ignored them.

"I asked you a question, Matt, and I want an answer," Ham repeated.

"Mom's just got a short fuse, Dad. I'm not doin' anything my friends don't do," Matt replied.

"That's not true," Ben protested. "He's been mean to everyone including his friends."

"Oh, shut up, Ben. You keep out of this. He didn't ask your opinion," Matt replied angrily.

"See, he is a jerk," Abby added. "Boy, are you gonna get it now."

Matt picked up a spoon and threw it at Abby. She ducked down and it hit the wall behind her. It fell making a clanging sound as it hit the floor.

"What is wrong with you, Matt?" Ham asked angrily. "You better get control of yourself, young crab. We don't act like that in my house."

"Can't you see she started it?" Matt argued. "She made me do it."

"No, she didn't, Matt," Ali said. "You made the choice to get upset. And you have been doing that a whole lot lately."

Matt jumped up out of his chair and declared, "Nobody understands me. I hate living in this family. You just don't get it." He forcefully pushed his chair aside knocking it over and hurried to his room. He slammed the door. The walls shuddered slightly.

"Well, Ham, so what do you think?" Ali asked. "Does that seem like normal behavior to you?"

Suddenly Ham appeared angry. "You act like it's my fault," he replied. "I didn't do anything to him. I think he's just pushing your hot buttons, and you're letting him do it. He's using you to get what he wants and you're playing along." Ham got up from the table, threw his napkin down and went to his study.

Ali sat dazed for a moment. "Why do I feel like I've been here before? Is this some sort of recurring nightmare?" she asked quietly. "Did I miss part of the conversation?"

Ben stopped eating. "No, Mom," Ben answered. "Dad says weird stuff too sometimes. I think they both have the same problem. Maybe they both came from outer space."

"I think they're from Mars or Jupiter," Abby offered.

"Maybe their spaceship will come back for them someday and take them home," Ben said with a grin.

"We can always hope," Abby replied sighing and gazing upward. "But for now, I'll help you clean up." She collected the dishes off of the table and helped her mother finish putting away the leftovers.

"I'm going to bed early," Ali said. "I'm worn out dealing with all of this."

CHAPTER 4
Nightmare Visitors

Ali didn't sleep well that night. She was awakened by the sound of Matt crying out in the middle of the night. She got up out of bed to see what he needed. She found him sleeping in his bed, but he was very restless. He was rolled up in his bed sheets rocking from side to side. Moonlight streamed brightly through his bedroom window. Ali could just make out the Power Lobster figure on his bedspread. As she looked around his room, she noticed that he had taken down so many of the posters that they had put up together only a year ago.

"Where's his Power Lobster poster? Where are the soccer and football posters?" she thought. "He had a nice signed poster we got for him at a football game just last year. And where are his soccer trophies?" All she could see were black walls covered with paper scraps, which were filled with unreadable writing scribbled on them. There were two photos of dragons dressed in solid black leather. "Something strange and awful is definitely happening to my child," she told herself.

"Matt, are you okay?" she asked softly. His eyes opened suddenly and he jumped up out of bed. Without warning, he rushed around his room in a circle three times while crying out.

"Get them off me. Get them off of me, Mom. Get them off of me," Matt cried. He was very agitated and waved his claws wildly in the air like he was batting at unseen attackers.

"Get what off of you, Matt?" she asked bewildered. "I

don't see anything." Ali held a claw out to halt Matt's motion so she could try to find his unseen attackers. She searched him but found nothing.

"Don't you see them? They're all over me! They're biting me! Do something, Mom! Help me!" Matt cried and was slapping at his legs.

"Matt, there's nothing on you. You're having a nightmare," Ali called to him hoping to awaken him. He continued to shriek and cry out. Finally Ali grabbed him with both claws and shook him hard. "Matt, please wake up," she pleaded. His eyes were glassy, and he appeared to be staring right through her. She was frightened. "Matt, wake up!" she cried loudly.

This startled Matt and suddenly he stopped crying and thrashing about. He looked at his mother. "Mom, what are you doing?" he asked. "You're hurting me."

Ali then realized that she had grabbed him very tightly and was shaking him. She released him from her grip. "I was trying to wake you up, Matt," she replied. "You scared the daylights out of me."

"What are you talking about?" Matt asked as he rubbed the marks her claws had left on his upper legs.

"You, Matt. You were running around screaming about something biting you. It scared me. Your eyes were wide open, but you were obviously not awake until now," she said.

"I don't remember anything, Mom."

"I'm sorry if I hurt you, but you scared me so badly; I was just trying to wake you up," Ali explained. "Let me see your legs." She tried to look at his legs, but he refused.

"It's no big deal, Mom," Matt said. "Can I go back to bed?"

"That sounds like a good idea," Ali agreed. She closed the door and shuffled back to her bedroom feeling weak and shaken. "This is so strange," she mumbled as she fell back asleep.

CHAPTER 5
The Sugar Monster

The next morning Matt was up early looking for something to eat. He banged the dark red wooden cupboards loudly as he searched for what he wanted.

"Matt, what are you doing?" Ben asked sleepily. He yawned and gently rubbed his eyes with his antennae.

"I'm hungry. Don't we have anything sweet to eat around here?" Matt asked grumpily.

"Well, there's frosted Krispy Buds," Ben offered.

"No, I want cookies or doughnuts or pancakes," Matt insisted and started banging the counters with his large claw. "Mom, I want some breakfast," he yelled. "Get up and fix me something."

Abby appeared. "Shut up, Matt and let mom get a little sleep," she replied. "Can't you get it yourself? Are your claws broken or something?"

Matt whirled around to face Abby. "You are so stupid. I ignore stupid little crabs like you," Matt replied angrily. Abby stamped the floor.

"Talk about stupid," Abby yelled back. "You're the one who's so stupid around here. I wish Mom and Dad would send you away to a boarding school or something."

A very sleepy momma crab appeared in the doorway. "Why are you two fighting? It's too early in the morning to fight. Can't you save it for a little later in the day so I can sell tickets?" Ali said with a slight grin. Everyone stopped and turned to look at her.

"Are you kidding, Mom?" Abby asked. She appeared very concerned. "I don't want strangers watching us fight."

"Of course she's kidding, Abby," Ben replied. "She's smiling, isn't she?" Abby breathed a sigh of relief.

"You are so stupid, Abby," Matt said mockingly. "You actually believed that Mom was gonna sell tickets?" He started to laugh very loudly.

"Stop it, Matt," Abby yelled and started to cry. Ali saw the situation was getting out of hand.

"Matt, please restrain yourself. If you want any breakfast, you'd better stop laughing right now," Ali demanded firmly. Matt stopped laughing and began to sulk. "Sit down at the table, and I'll fix you something to eat," she added.

Matt, Ben, and Abby sat down at the dark wooden dinner table.

"I want something sweet," Matt ordered loudly. "And I want it now."

Ali acted like she didn't hear Matt and started cooking bacon and eggs. The sizzling sound and pungent bacon smell tipped Matt off that she wasn't giving in to his demands.

"I said I wanted something sweet. Not bacon and eggs," Matt insisted.

Ali continued to ignore Matt's request. He jumped up from the table and slapped his mother hard on the back of her shell. She fell forward and almost dropped the pan of hot bacon grease.

"What is wrong with you, Matt?" Ali asked, surprised by his violent action. "I almost spilled hot grease on myself. I could've been badly burned."

"Well, you deserve it for ignoring me," Matt replied.

Ben and Abby jumped up from the table at the same time and forced Matt over into a corner of the room. "We are so tired of this, Matt," Ben declared angrily. "If you ever hit Mom again, I'll make you regret you were ever born."

"And I'll call the police," Abby answered. "I hope they put you in jail and throw away the key."

Ali had recovered her balance and calmed down. She set the hot grease aside. "Ben and Abby, come sit down and eat your breakfast," Ali requested. "I'm fine, and I'm sure that Matt didn't really mean what he said."

Ham appeared in the doorway. "What's all the commotion?" he asked.

"Matt hit Mom," Abby shouted.

"What?" Ham looked shocked. "Why did you hit your mother, Matt?"

Matt was cowering in the corner like a caged animal. "I, I didn't mean to," he whimpered. "She wouldn't fix me what I wanted for breakfast." Matt sobbed and shook.

"Give me a break," Ben laughed. "Matt did it on purpose. Poor little Matt didn't get his way so he hit Mom. Does that sound like a wonderful son?" Ben stalked off and roughly pushed Matt as he passed. "You're gonna get it," Ben whispered under his breath.

"Dad," Matt cried. "Ben threatened me."

"Go to your room, Ben," Ham ordered.

"With pleasure," Ben replied and hurried out.

"He really did do it on purpose, Dad," Abby reported. "Mom almost got burned with bacon grease because of Matt."

"Abby, please finish up your breakfast and go to your room," Ali requested. Abby nodded and carried her plate to the sink. She hurried to her room.

"Now tell me what really happened," Ham requested. Matt continued to whimper in the corner.

"Give it a rest, Matt," Ali replied. "Your audience is gone." Matt straightened up.

"Don't believe her," Matt said. "She just wants you to punish me."

"And why should I believe you and not your mother, Matt?" Ham asked. Matt suddenly drew into his shell.

"Matt, don't you hide from me," Ham called. He tapped on Matt's shell. "Come on out or you won't have any defense." Matt refused to answer and didn't come out. "What is wrong with him?" Ham asked.

"That's what I'd like to know," Ali answered.

"Can't you take him to the doctor?" he asked. "He's way too young to be acting so rebelliously; it has to be something else. So what did happen this morning?"

"Just one more knot in a string of events that tells me we are losing our son," she answered. "I just want to get some help for Matt. This is so much more than just bad behavior. Sometimes he acts like someone else has taken control of him. His eyes look glassy and far away. I'm not sure Matt is even in there."

"Well, I'm hungry," Ham said. "Can I get some breakfast?"

Ali shrugged.

"You aren't even listening," she muttered.

"And what about the soccer tournament? I'm supposed to help with the concessions today," Ham reminded.

"Oh, I almost forgot," Ali replied. "Ben, Abby, do you still want to go to the soccer tournament today?" she called. Ben and Abby came hurrying down the hallway.

"I need to go," Ben replied. "My team plays today."

"Me, too," Abby said. "We're in the tournament today."

"I'm not sure what to do about Matt," Ali said quietly. By this time Matt had emerged from his hiding and was sneaking his way down the back hall.

"I wanna go," Matt replied eagerly and bounded into the kitchen.

"Are you alright?" Ali asked. Matt nodded happily.

Ali shook her head with her claw up to her mouth and murmured, "I just don't get it."

"Well, then we need to hurry up and get ready," Ham replied. "I hate being late." He hurriedly ate the rest of his bacon and eggs and toast. Ali cleared the dishes and everyone else gathered up the soccer gear and loaded it into the car.

CHAPTER 6
Soccer Rage

The family car was speeding along toward the county soccer fields. The sky was bright and clear blue with a wispy white cloud or two. It was a perfect day for soccer.

"I hope we win," Abby remarked on the way to the soccer field. "My team plays first."

"You've got a pretty good chance," Ben noted. "Your team has been looking good the last few games."

"Who cares," Matt interrupted. "You girls look so dorky running around the field. And what a dorky name your team has. Who named you the 'Honey Bees' anyway?"

"Stop it, Matt," Ali's voice was tense. "I'm not going to listen to that." Matt crossed his claws and fell silent. They arrived in time for Abby to warm up with the team. Her team was ranked fourth in the league, and they hoped to move up during the tournament.

"We play later," Ben whispered to his mom. "I'm hungry. Can I go get something to eat?"

"Ben, you just ate breakfast not even an hour ago," Ali replied.

"Please, Mom, I'm a growing crab," Ben pleaded with a big grin.

"Yeah, you're growing, Ben. Bigger and bigger," Matt said and he laughed.

"Zip it, Matt," Ben shot back. "You don't have any room to talk. I hear you up eating in the middle of the night."

"It's because I can't sleep," Matt answered. "You don't have the nightmares that I have. I feel better when I get up and eat."

"Then don't make fun of me," Ben replied and headed for the concession stand.

Matt made a face at Ben as he walked to the concession stand. "He's such a dope," Matt mumbled.

"Matt, when does your team play?" Ali asked.

"I don't know," Matt answered. "I don't care about playing anyway."

"You're the one who wanted to come," she reminded him.

"That's so Dad wouldn't punish me for hitting you this morning," Matt revealed. "I think soccer is stupid."

"That's funny," Ali remarked. "You didn't think it was stupid when your team won first place last season. You seemed awfully proud of that trophy."

"That was last year, Mom," Matt replied. "Things are different now. I don't feel that way anymore."

"Oh really," she replied skeptically. "Well go check the times on the bulletin board anyway." Matt walked slowly over to the board, and he returned moving just as slowly.

"So when does your team play?" Ali asked again.

"We play late today," Matt replied. "That stinks. I've got to stay here and watch Dorky and Dumbbell play soccer before I finally get to play."

"That's okay," she replied. "Dorky and Dumbbell have to endure watching you play too."

"I'm gonna get something to eat," Matt said and wandered off to the concession stand. He found Ben eating a hotdog.

"Where'd you get the money for that?" Matt asked.

"Dad's working the stand," Ben replied. "Go ask him."

Matt got some nachos to eat and sat down across from Ben at a wooden picnic table stained with ketchup and mustard.

"So when do you play?" Matt asked.

"In about an hour," Ben answered with his mouth full. He swallowed the bite down. "What about you?"

"We don't play until after lunch," Matt answered. "What a bummer. I'm so bored."

"Why don't we go shoot some balls on a free field?" Ben asked.

"What does it matter? We're not gonna win anyway," Matt replied.

"That's not true," Ben said. "Your team won the finals last season."

"That doesn't mean we'll win this season," Matt replied.

"What's going on with you, Matt?" Ben asked. "You are so down on everything."

"It's none of your business," Matt answered and walked away.

Ben couldn't leave it alone. He followed Matt and got in front of him. "Matt, that's not good enough," Ben said. "You owe us an explanation for the way you've been acting lately. Are you taking drugs or drinkin' ?"

Matt started screaming and stamping the ground. "No, No I'm not! Leave me alone!"

"Okay, okay," Ben replied and backed away from Matt. "What a hothead," he murmured and walked back to where Ali was sitting.

Abby, as goalie, stood and watched the ball closely. As the ball advanced toward her goal area, she moved up quickly and batted it to a strong kicker who launched it back safely onto the other side of the field. Abby was able to keep the other team from scoring and the Honey Bees won the game 5-0. They advanced to the next round in the tournament.

Ben's team the Blue Rockets played on a larger field because they were older. His game started a few minutes before Abby's ended, but Ali waited until her game was over before going to watch Ben play.

"Congratulations, Abby," Ali said. "You looked sharp out there.

Abby beamed. "Thanks, Mom," she replied. "Can I get something to drink?"

"Dad's working the concession stand," she answered. "Get whatever you want. I'll move our stuff over to where Ben's team is playing. Come on over to field eight."

"Okay, Mom," Abby said and hurried to join her team- mates in line at the concession stand. The line of giggling young girls was loud and unruly.

"How'd you do?" Ham asked. He already had a good idea who won by their excited chatter and gestures.

"We won!" they all said at once.

"Congratulations, girls," he said. "I'm sure you played a fine game. What was the score?"

"Five to nothin'!" one of the girls answered loudly.

"That's great," he said with a big smile and a wink.

Ben's team played well, but struggled against a larger and faster team. Ben scraped his leg when he and another player ran into each other trying to kick the ball down the field. Ben limped off the field. The field nurse applied a bandage to stop the bleeding.

"You're hurt," one of his teammates noted.

"It's not that bad," Ben replied. "I almost had the goal."

"Be still until it stops bleeding," the nurse ordered.

"Yes, Ma'am," Ben replied and lay back on the grass. Ali came over to check on Ben.

"How's your leg, Ben?" Ali asked. "You took a pretty hard hit."

"It's okay," Ben replied. He wasn't able to play the rest of the game due to his injury. His team lost 2-3. After the game, Ben limped over to where Ali and Abby were sitting.

"Oh well," Ben said. "We tried our best. They just played better." He sat down next to Abby. "You played a good game, Abby."

"Thanks," Abby said and smiled. "We play again this afternoon."

"I hope your team wins again," Ben replied. He put his claw around her and gave her a hug. Abby smiled.

After lunch, the family moved to another field to watch Matt's team play. Matt moved slower than usual. He couldn't seem to keep up with the other players. When he had the ball, the other players quickly stole it away from him. He was getting very frustrated. He set up to block a ball and it hit him on the side of the head. He dropped down and started to cry. The game stopped as everyone kneeled down, and the coach rushed out to check on him.

"Are you okay, Matt?" the coach asked.

"No, I'm not," Matt yelled back. "I'm gonna kill that crab who kicked the ball at me." Matt jumped up and started rushing toward the soccer player from the other team who had kicked the ball. A look of horror came upon the other crab's face as Matt came steaming across the field like a wild bull. "I'm gonna kill you!" he screamed. "You hurt me on purpose!"

The player quickly drew up into his blue and green spiral shell. Matt started kicking the outside of his shell. "I hate you," he yelled. Players and coaches rushed over to pull Matt away from the frightened crab.

"He tried to hurt me," Matt screamed. "You saw him. He did it on purpose."

Ali hurried over to pull Matt away from the confused and angry crowd. "He's not feeling well," she said. "He needs to sit down and rest. After all, he was hit on the head."

The coach came over red-faced and upset. "I can't have a crazy crab going around attacking other players like that," he barked. "We're sure to get a penalty for that little incident."

"I'm sorry," Ali answered. "He doesn't need to play anymore today."

"I'm not sure when he can play again," the coach replied.

Ali ushered Matt over to where the rest of the family was sitting. "Matt, are you hurt?" she asked. Matt was sobbing and shaking. He shook his head and pulled up into his shell. "You'll be okay, sweetheart. We love you."

Matt's team went on to win the game 7-4 despite his angry outburst and violent attack on the other team's player. Since he had been ejected by the coach, they didn't have to forfeit the game. Abby's team played again that afternoon and won their second game 5-2.

"We play again tomorrow for the championship," Abby said with a gleam in her eyes.

Ali nodded. "We'll bring you back to play tomorrow," she said. "Let's pack up and go home. Dad should be finishing up at the concession stand by now." When they arrived home, Ali was feeling too tired to cook.

"Let's order pizza," Abby suggested.

"Okay with me," Ham replied. "What does everyone else want? Mom?"

"Pizza sounds fine," she replied wearily.

Abby enjoyed placing the order over the phone. "It'll be ready in about twenty minutes," Abby called. "We are going to pick it up, aren't we, Dad? I told the pizza man we would pick it up."

"Yes, Abby, I'll pick it up," Ham answered. After dinner, Abby, Ben and Matt piled onto the old blue couch and decided to watch TV together, so that Ali and Ham could have some time to talk alone.

"I'm really worried about Matt," Ali told Ham. "He practically got kicked off the team today."

"What are you talking about?" he asked. "What happened?"

"Well, he was hit by a soccer ball on the head during the game, and he went crazy. He started threatening the little crab who kicked the ball and ran at him like an angry bull. I was afraid he was going to hurt him," she continued.

"So what happened after that?" Ham asked.

She cleared her throat and continued, "The little crab hid in his shell and Matt started beating on it. The coaches had to pull Matt off. I had to rescue him from the crowd. They kicked him out of the game and possibly the rest of the season. He really frightened everyone including me."

"You've got to take him to the doctor and soon," Ham insisted.

"I plan to," she replied. "I've got an appointment scheduled for him next week. I just hope I can make it until then. I'm exhausted. It's been a stressful day."

He nodded. "You need to get some rest, dear," he said and gave her a kiss.

CHAPTER 7
The Fruity Fiasco

Ali awoke to the rain pitter pattering on the window. She watched as the water formed tiny rivers running down the window pane. "There must've been a storm last night," she thought. Ali found Matt asleep on her bedroom floor. The blue carpet had irregular impressions where the children had slept on stormy nights in the past. All three had a fear of thunderstorms, and she always allowed them to come to her room if they were afraid. But Matt had become an almost nightly visitor. He was so afraid to be alone at night. It started several months ago and no matter what she said to reassure him, Matt still felt safer sleeping in their room. She quietly got up and went to the kitchen to start breakfast. The food was cooking nicely and the air was fragrant with the smell of pancakes, butter and syrup.

"Ummm," Ben said as he came in. "What smells so good, Mom?"

"Pancakes, dear. Would you like some?" she asked and pointed to a freshly cooked pancake in the skillet.

"Yes, please," Ben said nodding his antennae vigorously. He sat down at the table and began eating hungrily.

Abby appeared next. "Oh, Mom, you're wonderful," she said. "I want two pancakes with lots of syrup."

"Have a seat," Ali answered and served up two fresh hot pancakes on Abby's plate. Abby moved her seat next to Ben's and sat down.

"Pass the butter and syrup please, Ben," Abby said cheerfully. She hummed a happy tune and started pouring the warm syrup on her pancakes.

Ham wandered in looking very sleepy. "Those look good. I'm ready for some breakfast," he said.

"Have a seat, dear," Ali said. Ham found an empty spot and sat down. She served up two more fresh, hot pancakes.

"Is Matt still asleep?" Ali asked.

Ham nodded. "I think so."

"Matt...Matt, time for breakfast," Ali called. No one answered. "Matt, please come join us for breakfast," she called louder. When there continued to be no answer, Ali looked around. "Ben, you're about finished with breakfast. Could you go get your brother up, please? He's on our bedroom floor."

"Okay," Ben replied and disappeared into the bedroom. Moments later, he came rushing back into the room with Matt in hot pursuit. Matt slammed into the doorway with his large claw. It caused the dishes to rattle. He appeared very angry with his claws open ready to attack.

"Mom, stop Matt. He threatened to hurt me," Ben cried as he hurried around the table to get away from Matt.

"Stop it, Matt! Have a seat and eat some breakfast," Ali ordered. "Put your claws in or I'll let you see what mine feel like."

"He yelled at me," Matt said angrily.

"So what?" she answered. "I told Ben to wake you up and tell you to come eat pancakes with the rest of the family."

"He scared me," Matt cried. "I don't want any of your stupid pancakes."

"Okay, we'll eat them all by ourselves. I was just trying to be nice, but I'm not going to wait for you to get in the mood to eat. You're part of this family, and I expect you to eat with the rest of us," Ali answered. She was very annoyed by Matt's behavior.

"I'll eat some of your dumb ole pancakes," Matt relented.

Ali decided to ignore Matt's rude comment.

"So what time is your game today, Abby?" Ali asked. "One-thirty," Abby replied.

"Good, we'll have time to get back from church and eat lunch before we have to leave," Ali said. "We need to get ready to go to church as soon as you're finished with breakfast."

Things went smoothly at church. On the way home Ali remembered that she needed to stop by the grocery store. Matt insisted on going in with her.

"Just stay in the car, Matt. I'll only be a few minutes," Ali requested.

"No, I wanna go too," Matt whined. Ali gave in to keep him from making a scene. Had she known what was about to happen inside the store, she would have insisted he stay in the car.

Matt wandered down the produce aisle and had to touch and handle everything. He dropped a couple of pieces of fruit and Ali was not happy about it.

"Matt, please stop touching everything. You've dropped two things already, and I don't want to have to buy everything in the store because you broke it or dropped it on the floor," Ali chided.

"There you go picking on me again," Matt announced loudly. He started screaming and crying and throwing the produce. Ali ducked to miss being hit.

"Stop it, Matt. There is no reason for you to behave like this." She moved to block his next throw and took a direct

hit on the front of her shell. He continued to throw fruit at her until the manager of the store came to see what all the commotion was about.

"What seems to be the problem, Ma'am?" he asked. The look on his face was one of shock and disapproval.

"My son and I are having a disagreement," Ali replied and proceeded to wipe the smashed cherries off her shell.

"You will be charged for those I hope you know," he continued.

"I had assumed so," she replied. "Will there be a cleaning charge as well?"

"No, Ma'am," he answered.

"Good," Ali replied. She turned her head and in a funny tone of voice shouted, "Clean up, Aisle 3!" The manager had to hold back a chuckle at her sense of humor.

Meanwhile Matt was hitting Ali and cursing at her; he knew this really bothered and embarrassed her. Passing

shoppers appeared offended and some just stopped and stared at the scene in disbelief.

"What's wrong with him?" one lady crab asked.

"I don't know," Ali answered.

"You need to discipline him more," a large red lobster commented. "He's obviously spoiled."

One great blue heron said, "Some parent you are. I can't believe you're letting him act that way. You should be ashamed of yourself. Doesn't he have a father who knows how to spank him?"

Matt's mom reared back on her hind legs and proclaimed, "I am not a bad parent and yes, his father does know how to discipline him, but spanking is not the answer to his behavior. And I would appreciate it if you'd mind your own business." Ali finished as much of her shopping as she could and herded Matt out the door before anyone else could say anything to them. She was embarrassed and angry, not at Matt, but at the judgment of total strangers who had no idea what her life was like living with Matt's mood swings and temper tantrums.

Once in the car, she felt the tears sting her antennae. They splashed down the front of her shell and onto the seat. "I'll never take him to the store again as long as I live," she thought.

"Mom, are you alright?" Abby asked.

Ali brushed away the remaining tears and nodded. "Yes, dear, I'm just a little stressed," she replied. Ali took a deep breath and let it out very slowly.

"What took so long?" Ben asked.

"What took so long?" Matt mocked Ben. "And wouldn't you like to know, Mr. Nosey Pants?"

"Stop it, Matt," Ali ordered firmly. "We had a little problem, Ben. It's under control now."

She drove home silently. The usual bickering of her children seemed so far away, and she felt like she was living in a dream, a very bad dream. She fixed lunch for everyone and tried very hard to look happy, but she felt very frightened and desperate inside. When it was time to go to Abby's soccer game, she just couldn't find the energy to go.

"Mom, it's time to go," Abby said.

Ali sighed heavily. "I'm too tired. Ham, can you take her? I just don't feel very good."

Ham nodded and pointed Abby to the car. "Are you okay, Hon?" he asked.

"I just don't know how much more of this I can take with Matt. I don't know if my sanity will last until his doctor's appointment," she answered. "Those shoppers in the store were so thoughtless and unkind. Passing judgment on me without even knowing my child or my situation. It really hurts." Tears began to flow again, and she didn't try to stop them this time. "Sometimes I feel like I'm losing my mind. I feel as if I'm living in a war zone trying not to step on a landmine."

"You get some rest, dear, and I'll take Ben and Abby with me. Do you want me to take Matt too?" he asked.

"Matt, do you want to go see Abby's game today or stay home with me?" Ali called. No one answered. She got up from the couch and knocked on his door. Still there was no answer. She opened the door and found him curled up and sound asleep on the floor.

"I guess that answers your question," Ham said chuckling and headed for the back door. She lay down on the couch and fell asleep.

Ali awoke when she felt someone nudging her. Matt was standing beside the couch staring at her with his face very close to hers.

"Matt, what are you doing?" she asked startled.

"Momma, you are so beautiful. I want to kiss you like daddy does. Can I?" Matt asked. His voice was very dreamy, so smooth and mellow.

"Who is this lovey dovey Matt and where did he come from?" she thought. "I'm so confused."

"No, Matt," she answered. "Kissing like that can spread germs, and I don't want you to get sick. Besides I don't kiss Ben or Abby like that and they never complain."

"But I want to know about the love you and daddy have. And I want to know where baby crabs come from," Matt said and cocked his antennae, ready for Ali to explain everything to him.

"Well, I hate to let you down, but you are just too young to learn about those things right now," Ali replied. "When you are old enough, I'll tell you, but not yet. Okay?" Matt nodded slowly. His look of excitement changed quickly to disappointment and hurt. He went silently to his room with his head hanging down. Ali headed off to her bedroom to lie down, but it disturbed her that Matt seemed so upset when she denied his request. She couldn't rest and decided to get up and check on him. She found him in his room wrapped up in his Power Lobster blanket facing the wall.

"Matt, you understand that there are certain times when showing affection is okay and other times when it's not?" Ali asked as she reached over to gently touch the back of his shell with her claw.

Matt rolled over suddenly. His face was very angry.

"Yeah, I understand," he replied hatefully. "Don't ever touch me again or I'll call the police." Shocked by Matt's words, Ali pulled away and hurried out the door. Tears were streaming silently down her antennae.

It was past dinner time when Ham, Ben and Abby got home. The Honey Bees had won the tournament and Abby held her trophy tightly.

"Look, Mom," Abby called excitedly. "We won. Look at my trophy."

Ali was sitting on the couch reading. She set her book aside and admired the gold and red sculpture. It sported a large golden soccer ball on top of a round pedestal. The lower portion was square and had a gold plate with an inscription. The inscription read "2001 Champions". Mom nodded. "Very nice, Abby. You girls did a great job. I'm very proud of you."

Abby beamed and held her trophy up high over her head. She chanted, "We are the champions."

Ben and Ham followed with the soccer gear. Ben headed for his room. "You did good, champ," he called over his back.

"They played well," Ham commented as he stood next to the couch. "Abby really did a great job. It came down to a shoot out, and she shut them out as the goalie. I was proud." He patted Abby on the back of her shell. She smiled.

"Why don't you get cleaned up and ready for dinner, Abby?" Ali requested. Abby nodded and happily danced off to her room still singing.

"Any problems with Matt?" Ham asked.

"Well," she replied. "He did act a little odd, but nothing surprises me anymore. I did get some rest."

"Are you feeling any better?" he asked.

"Yes, I'm not as tired now. I wonder how Matt is feeling?" Ali replied. "I guess we'll find out soon enough."

Ali got up to fix dinner. She found herself dreading Matt waking up. Then she felt guilty for feeling that way. Fortunately the smells of dinner woke Matt up, and he came to the dinner table on his own. He was in a better mood than he had been in for several days.

"So who won the soccer tournament?" Matt asked cheerfully. Everyone paused.

Finally Ben answered. "Abby's team won 1st place."

"That's nice," Matt replied. "Did you get a trophy, Abby?"

"Yeah," Abby answered nodding. Everyone was prepared for Matt's angry or insulting words, but they never came. They never came during dinner or the rest of the evening. Matt seemed to have changed back into a nice crab. Ham felt this proved that he was just acting out to upset his mother. Ali knew something far more serious was going on. Ben and Abby wondered how long the nice Matt would last. So maybe Matt wasn't really an alien after all or was he just pretending?

CHAPTER 8
Super Crab

"It's time to go," Ali announced. She gathered up school books and placed them in backpacks. "Come on, gang. It's time to leave."

Ben came out of his room. Abby followed him down the hall. "Do we have to go to school, Mom? I'm tired," Abby complained.

"Yes, Abby," Ali replied as she gave Abby her backpack. "You have to go to school. Yesterday the champion, but today it's back to school."

Abby shrugged and frowned. Ben snickered with his claw up to his face.

"Don't feel bad, Abby," Ben said. "You could take your trophy and show it off at school today."

"Good idea," Abby replied as her face brightened.

"Where's Matt?" Ali asked. The door suddenly opened slamming against the wall and Matt jumped into the hallway.

"Never fear; Super Crab is here!" Matt exclaimed. He had a sheet hooked over the edge of his shell like a cape and raced up the hallway making whooshing sounds like he was flying. "I will save the world from destruction. Move aside earth crabs. I have work to do," Matt said in a deep dramatic tone of voice.

"What in the world?" Ali said with her claw over her mouth.

"Matt, you look weird," Abby said and started giggling.

"Matt, we have to go to school," Ben reminded and stepped in front of Matt to stop him. Matt ran into Ben and fell back against the wall.

"What are you doing, earth crab?" Matt asked. "How dare you stop me on my mission to save Earth from alien invaders? Get out of my way or I will have to destroy you. I have laser vision and super strength so step aside or die."

"Matt, cut it out," Ben answered. "You're not funny. We have to go to school. Take that stupid sheet off and let's get going." Ben tried to pull the sheet off of Matt's shell.

Matt jumped up and rammed Ben as hard as he could. Ben fell roughly against the wall making a hole in it with his shell. The house shuddered from the impact.

"You will not stop me. You cannot stop me, foolish earth crab. For I am Super Crab," Matt shouted. Matt ran to the

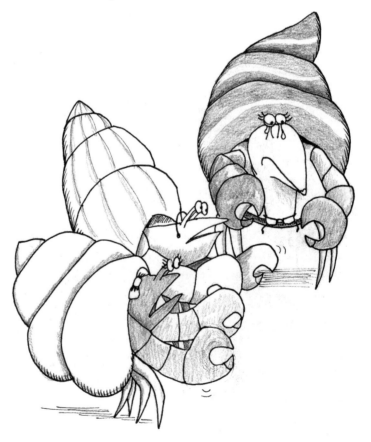

window and climbed up on the window sill. He pulled open the window before anyone could stop him. Ali was becoming very alarmed.

"Matt, please stop it," she pleaded. "Please come down out of the window or you'll hurt yourself." She tried to grab Matt's shell.

"Let go of me. I must fly off to stop the aliens this instant," Matt called and batted at his mother's claw holding him. He was pulling against it trying to jump out of the window.

"Hurry, Ben, I'm afraid he's going to hurt himself. I can't hold him much longer," Ali called behind her. Ben struggled

up and rushed over. He grabbed the other side of Matt's shell as he was trying to push away from the window sill. It caused Matt to fall back into the room. Matt, Ali, and Ben tumbled backward.

Abby was screaming, "Are you alright? Are you alright?" She was checking on Ali and helping her up. Ali was a little dizzy, but she was able to stand up.

"I'm okay," Ali said. "Ben, Matt are you boys okay?"

"I'm fine, Mom," Ben replied. "I'm not so sure about Super Crab. He looks a little pale."

Matt had been thrown down pretty hard, and it had the knocked the wind out of him. "I'm okay," he gasped. Matt was back in touch with reality.

Abby came over and asked, "Are you Matt or Super Crab?"

"That's a stupid question, bean brain," he answered in his normal voice.

"At least the mean old Matt is back," Abby giggled. "But Super Crab was kind of cute."

"What are you talking about?" Matt asked. "And what's this stupid sheet doing on my shell?"

"Forget it," Ali replied quickly. "Matt, I'm not sure that you should go to school today. I'm afraid that you might lose control."

"I'm okay, Mom," Matt assured. "I'll be good. I promise. I don't know what happened to me, but I'm okay now."

Ali was so tired of his behavior. She needed a break. "I can't wait any longer. I'm going to take you to see the doctor today, so I'll pick you up early," she replied. "I'd better drive you to school or you'll be late." They hurried to get to school before the tardy bell rang.

§

Ali arrived at school to pick up Matt and take him to see Dr. Tory. When she got to school, Matt was in the office. He was sitting with his face in his claws.

"What's wrong, Matt?" Ali asked. "Tell me what happened." Matt shook his head and refused to answer.

"Are you Ms. Lavar?" the assistant principal asked.

"Yes, I am," Ali replied.

"I'm Ms. Rolle, the assistant principal," she said.

"Nice to meet you," Ali said. "What has happened?"

Ms. Rolle was a tall great land crab with long and slender bluish-white legs. Her round black eyes were set close together on the front in shallow sockets. Her bluish-gray shell was flat on top and rounded underneath where her legs and claws were. She had two large and unequal claws.

"Matt lost his temper today. He attacked a little crab for spilling ketchup on him accidentally. Fortunately no one was hurt, but the little boy crab was really frightened by Matt's behavior," Ms. Rolle explained.

"You said the little boy is okay?" Ali asked.

"Yes," Ms. Rolle replied. "But I don't want it to happen again."

"I'm taking him to the doctor today to try and find out what's going on with him. He has been acting very strangely and we're not sure what's wrong. Hopefully the doctor will be able to help us," she said.

"That sounds like a good plan," Ms. Rolle replied and jotted down a note on her notepad.

CHAPTER 9
Doctor Tory

"Matt, please follow me," the nurse requested. She was a small green bullfrog and hopped down the hallway leading Matt and Ali into an exam room.

"The doctor will be with you shortly," the nurse said as she closed the door. She disappeared and the room grew quiet. Matt glanced around the exam room. The walls were painted sea green and on them hung pictures of happy little crabs, lobsters, sea gulls, pelicans, turtles and frogs playing together.

"How boring," he thought. "Why do I have to come see

a dumb doctor?"

Soon Dr. Tory came in the room. Dr. Tory, a pelican, was very large and stocky. He had light brown feathers and a long flat yellowish bill. His head was pale yellow and his neck was dark brown. His webbed feet slapped the floor loudly as he waddled into the room.

"Hello, Matt, I'm Dr. Tory," he said. "What seems to be the problem today?"

Matt sat motionless. He didn't say a word. He stared into space.

"Matt, tell the doctor what's wrong," Ali prompted. Matt remained silent. After a few minutes, the doctor turned his gaze toward Ali.

"Okay, I'll tell you, Doctor," Ali began. "I wanted to give

Matt a chance, but since he isn't talking, I'll tell you my side of the story. Matt has been acting very strangely, Dr. Tory. He has been very moody and emotional. He rages and screams; he throws things and hits his family. He thinks he is a super hero one minute trying to fly out the window and is terribly depressed the next. He attacked a crab at school today for accidentally spilling ketchup on him. He's punched holes in my walls, broken my dishes, and even threw food at me in the grocery store the other day. He has terrible nightmares and seems to be awake even when he's still asleep. He craves sugar all the time and stays up all night eating sweets. Sometimes he sleeps too much, and at other times he doesn't sleep at all. He is very angry and irritable most of the time. On rare occasions, we catch a glimpse of the old Matt, but most of the time he is this terribly angry crab who holds us hostage in a war zone. We are at our wit's end. He is destroying our family."

Dr. Tory tried to jot down what she was saying, but her words came so quickly he couldn't write fast enough. "So, you are having problems with Matt's behavior," Dr. Tory said trying to summarize.

"It's much more than just his behavior. There is something terribly wrong with Matt, Doctor. He has completely changed over the past few months. We don't even know him anymore, and we are very frightened of him. You never know what to expect from him. He may be happy and giddy or angry and insulting. Or like today. Silent. This is not normal," Ali informed him.

"So what would you like me to do?" Dr. Tory asked.

"Well what do you think is wrong with him, Doctor?" Ali asked.

"He doesn't seem to be a threat to himself or others right now so I don't see any need to hospitalize him. He may just need some counseling. I could run some blood tests, but I don't think his condition is serious. It sounds like he has an emotional adjustment disorder," Dr. Tory suggested. "We'll check him back in a month."

"A month!" Ali exclaimed. "Didn't you hear me? He's in trouble at home and at school. He's using his family as a punching bag, and we're getting tired of it. I think he is a threat to himself and others. A month is too long to wait for a return visit. This is serious, Doctor!"

"Stop by the lab and someone will draw his blood. My nurse will call you with the test results in a couple of days," Dr. Tory responded. "If there is a problem, I'll see him back then. Otherwise let me see him back in two weeks. Make a follow-up appointment before you leave."

On the drive home, Matt still wasn't talking.

"Okay, Matt, you can break your code of silence now," she said.

"I don't feel like talking," Matt replied.

"Well, you have some explaining to do, young crab," Ali said. "Why did you attack that crab at school today?"

"I don't know," Matt groaned. "He was annoying me with his ketchup. He was so loud and he wouldn't stop talking and laughing. I asked him to stop, but he just got louder and louder. He was waving the ketchup packet in my face and I tried to grab it. When I did, it exploded in my face. Something exploded in my head too. I'm not sure what happened after that. I know I knocked him down. I just wanted him to leave me alone," Matt explained. She knew he was telling the truth. Matt was just as confused by his feelings and mood swings as the rest of the family. He didn't like what he had become.

"Momma, I get so scared sometimes. I get a thought in my head, and I can't make it go away. It's like I have a video tape going inside my head. I keep having flashbacks of bad things happening over and over again, and I can't stop them. I just want to hold my head and make the pictures stop," he cried softly. Ali reached over and hugged him.

"I love you, and I will always be here for you," she said through her tears.

"I know, Mom" Matt replied. "I know you will."

CHAPTER 10
Alien Invasion

The red and orange rays of sunset streamed across the water's surface. They danced and shimmered atop the lapping waves. Abby was swinging on the tire swing. Ben was climbing up the rope tied to another limb of the tree when Ali and Matt arrived home from the doctor's office.

"Ben, what do you want to be when you grow up?" Abby asked.

Ben laughed. "Can't you guess, Abby?" Ben questioned. "I want to be an astronaut. I want to go into space some day."

"Oh," Abby replied. "You're right. I should've guessed."

"What about you?" Ben asked. "Do you know what you'd like to be?"

Abby stopped the tire swing. She climbed out and walked over and sat down facing the ocean. "I don't know, Ben," she said thoughtfully. "There are so many things I'd like to be. There are so many places I'd like to go and so many things I'd like to see. I think I'll just keep dreaming about them for now and not decide just yet."

Ben jumped down off the rope and sat down beside Abby.

"That's a really good answer," Ben replied. "Maybe I've decided too quickly about what I want to do. Being open about the future is good. You're pretty smart for a dumb little sister." Ben grinned and giggled. Abby pushed him over and threw sand on him. She went into the house.

After dinner, Matt and Ben decided to play basketball with the neighborhood kids. Abby was watching TV. Ali and Ham were in the study talking.

"So what did the doctor say?" Ham asked. Ali looked disgusted and discouraged.

"Precious little," she answered. "He thinks Matt has an emotional adjustment problem. Whatever that is. All I know is he didn't take me seriously."

"Did he run any tests?" Ham asked.

"Yes," Ali replied. "And we're supposed to go back in two weeks. I don't know if I can wait that long."

"Oh Honey. I'm not too worried about you," he reassured her.

"Maybe so," she said. "But will Matt last that long? His mood swings seem to be getting worse, and his behavior is more and more out of control."

Ham shook his head. "I don't know," he replied quietly. "I sure hope so."

The morning sky was gray and gloomy with the clouds dark and thick. Rain was definitely in the forecast. The morning sun couldn't seem to break through the darkness of the storm clouds to give light to the waiting beach below. And Ali couldn't seem to wake her sleeping crew and get them ready for school.

"Abby, Ben, Matt...Wake up," Ali called. "It's time to get up for school. Breakfast is ready and time's a wastin' as Granny used to say." Moans and groans greeted her cheerful morning summons. Ali continued to call and her persistence finally paid off. Three sleepy-eyed young crabs gathered around the breakfast table. "Cereal, oatmeal or French toast?" Ali asked.

"French toast," Abby answered, "with syrup and butter."

"Cereal is fine," Ben replied and reached to get the carton of milk. Matt just sat in his seat without a word.

"Matt," his mother asked, "what do you want to eat?" Still Matt didn't answer. She wasn't sure whether to pick something for him or continue waiting for a response. "How about French toast with syrup? It's sweet." Ali suggested. "Come on, Matt, help me." Her cheerful mood was fading fast. "Matt, are you in there?" she called loudly.

Matt's head snapped around. "Why are you yelling at me?" he screamed. "Why do you always treat me like I'm deaf or crazy? What's wrong with you, Mom? You're always so mean and hateful to me. You always pick on me. You don't treat Abby or Ben that way. You're nice to them. I see those things. You think I don't notice, but I do. You never really wanted me. You're sorry I was ever born. Aren't you? You hate me. You wish I would just go away or die or something. Don't you? Don't you?"

Ali was speechless with her mouth open. "That's not true, Matt," she finally choked out. "Your father and I…"

"Oh shut up. I don't want to hear your lies," Matt interrupted angrily. "Your father and I love you," he squeaked out in a high-pitched little voice mocking her. "Do you think anyone really believes you? You're probably planning to poison me. What's in the French toast anyway? Why are you trying to make me eat it? Watch out, Abby. Mom's trying to kill us."

Ben jumped up. "Matt, you're insane," he said. "Mom would never hurt us. I'm more afraid of you than anybody else in this house."

"Matt, you're scaring me," Abby said and started to cry.

She ran to her mother and hid behind her.

"Matt, go to your room," Ali ordered. Matt left the table and went to his room. Ali, Abby and Ben all breathed a sigh of relief.

"I don't know how much longer I can let this go on," Ali said quietly with her head down on the table. Abby and Ben finished breakfast and got ready for school. Ali went to check on Matt. When she opened his door, he was sitting on his bed reading a book.

"Matt, are you ready for school?" she asked carefully.

Matt looked up. "Sure, Mom," he replied cheerfully. He closed the book, set it on his desk, and put on his backpack.

"Are you hungry?" she asked.

"I'll just grab a piece of toast on the way out. Thanks, Mom," Matt answered. Matt seemed to be back to normal again. She was relieved.

Ali drove the kids to school because the weather looked so threatening. Matt's mood seemed calm.

§

Ms. Kay was reading the Thanksgiving story about the Pilgrims and the Indians during story time. The class was circled around her on a colorful patchwork rug as she rocked in her rocking chair. She described the Pilgrims' first difficult winter in great detail and how the friendly Indians who lived there showed them how to survive.

"They all celebrated their survival by sharing a meal together," said Ms. Kay. "We still celebrate it today. It's called Thanksgiving."

As Ms. Kay looked back down at her book, she became

aware of someone standing in front of her.

"I know who you really are! You are an alien!" a shrill voice exclaimed. Matt's claw was very close to Ms. Kay's face. All the children backed away from Matt, but he didn't move his claw from Ms. Kay's face.

"Matt, what's the matter?" Ms. Kay asked calmly and quietly.

"It's you, Ms. Kay and all of you," he said dropping his claw and pointing around the room. Ms. Kay breathed a sigh of relief when he moved his claw away from her face. "I'll get all of you. I'll find a way to stop you from taking over the world. You're all aliens, aren't you? I'll find a way to kill every one of you. I won't let you destroy us," Matt screamed. All the class scattered to hide from Matt. Ms. Kay was very frightened. She had to think of something quickly to distract Matt and get him away from the class.

"Matt, come quick," Ms. Kay called as she hurried outside the door. "I'm not really an alien. I'm a secret agent made to look like one. Follow me, and I'll show you how to be safe." Matt followed Ms. Kay who was signaling with her wing for him to come. By now she realized that something was wrong with Matt's mind and his thought processes; he didn't seem to know the difference between what was real and what wasn't.

"What's your plan, Ms. Kay?" Matt asked breathing hard.

"I need to get you to some place where you'll be safe," Ms. Kay said. "The clinic was safe before wasn't it?"

"Well, yes," Matt replied. "But I can't stop the aliens…"

"Yes, you can, Matt," Ms. Kay answered. "The aliens draw their energy from you and if you aren't around, they will start to die."

"Oh," Matt replied. "Then being in the clinic will hurt them?"

"Yes," Ms. Kay said. This calmed Matt down, and he walked to the clinic quietly. Ms. Kay hurried into the office and found Ms. Rolle. "Ms. Rolle, I have a child who I believe is a danger to himself and others. I'm not sure what to do. I have him in the clinic now. He is convinced we are all aliens that have come to take over the planet," Ms. Kay said.

"What did you say?" Ms. Rolle asked. "The child thinks we're aliens?" Ms. Kay nodded.

"But that's crazy. I've never heard of such a thing," Ms. Rolle continued. She followed Ms. Kay into the clinic. When they arrived, Matt was reading a library book.

"Matt," Ms. Rolle asked, "how are you feeling?"

Matt looked up and smiled. "Just fine, Ms. Rolle. How are you today?" he asked.

"What book are you reading?" Ms. Rolle asked.

"*Our Schoolteacher is an Alien,*" replied Matt. "It's really good."

"Matt, do you think that Ms. Kay and your classmates are aliens?" Ms. Rolle asked.

"That's a funny question, Ms. Rolle. Why would I think that? This is just a book. I know if something is real or not. Do you think I'd be hangin' around here if I thought they were aliens?" Matt asked.

Ms. Rolle motioned for Ms. Kay to step outside the room. "He seems to be okay now," Ms. Rolle noted. "Maybe it's just the book he's reading. That is an odd title for a book. Maybe he just has a wild and colorful imagination."

"I'm not convinced," Ms. Kay replied. "He sure acted as though he believed we were aliens in my classroom fifteen minutes ago. I want him to stay in the clinic with someone watching him until I can contact his mother."

"Who did you have in mind to watch him?" Ms. Rolle asked.

"I think the clinic mom will be safe, but she needs to stay just outside the room," Ms. Kay answered.

"Ms. Kay, Ms. Kay," Matt called. Ms. Kay and Ms. Rolle stepped back into the clinic room.

"Yes, Matt, what do you need?" Ms. Kay asked.

"Please may I go back to the room now?" Matt asked. Ms Rolle had an all-knowing look on her face as she peered at Ms. Kay.

"All right, I'll take him back to my room, but if he acts up again…" Ms. Kay cautioned.

"I'll be glad to deal with the situation," Ms. Rolle said. Ms. Kay took Matt back to her class. No one would sit near him or talk to him the rest of the day.

§

"Matt, it's time for dinner," Ali called. Abby and Ben were seated at the table. Ham was still in his study.

"Ham, could you check on Matt for me?" she requested. "We're ready to eat."

"Sure," Ham replied. He walked down the hallway and knocked on Matt's door. "Matt, it's time for dinner." There was no response. "Matt, I said it's time to eat," Ham repeated louder. He tried to turn the door knob, but it wouldn't budge. "This door doesn't have a lock," he thought. "Matt, open this door right now!" Ham was shouting now and quite upset. Ali had left the kitchen and joined Ham outside Matt's door.

"Matt, what's wrong? Please open the door," Ali pleaded. Faint crying could be heard through the door. "Something's wrong. He's in trouble. We've got to get in and help him," she said.

"Matt, is there something blocking the door?" Ham asked. The crying grew louder. Still Matt didn't answer. "I may have to break the door down."

"Go ahead," Ali said. "If you don't do it soon, I will." By now Abby and Ben had joined their mom and dad at Matt's door.

"What's going on, Mom?" Ben asked.

"Where's Matt?" Abby added. "And who's that crying?" By now the crying was easier to hear. It had become a sorrowful moaning sound.

"He's in his room," Ali replied. "Your dad is trying to get the door open. It seems to be locked or jammed."

"But, Mom, the door doesn't lock," Ben advised.

"Ham get a crowbar or something. We need to get to Matt," Ali insisted. "Can we take the doorknob out?"

"That's a good idea," Ham noted. "Ben go get my hammer and a screwdriver. No, just get my whole tool box."

"Sure, Dad," Ben answered and hurried to get the tools. When Ben returned, Ham was able to remove the doorknob and latch and then force the door open. Once it was opened, Ham discovered why he had been unable to open it. Matt had wedged the knob and placed every movable item in front of the door to block it. As the group pushed and pulled things away, they found Matt hiding under his bed.

"Matt, what are you doing?" Ali asked. "Why did you block the door?" Matt was sobbing hysterically.

"Matt, answer your mother," Ham ordered. Matt's eyes darted back and forth. He looked terrified. The scene frightened Ali so much that she began to weep. When Matt saw his mother's tears, he started to relax.

"Mom, you're not an alien," Matt said slowly.

"Of course not, dear," she replied. "Why on earth would you think I'm an alien?"

Matt dropped his head into his claws. "It was awful. I was surrounded by them. It's their eyes. They can't cry because they don't have real eyes. They've taken over the school. Ms. Kay tried to make me believe she wasn't one, but I never saw her cry," he explained. He raised his head up and looked at his mother. "They'll kill us and take over our bodies if we don't stop them. We have to stop them. We have to find a way to kill them. We have to find a way to keep them from taking over our bodies."

Ali cried at Matt's distressing revelation. Abby and Ben were shocked and dismayed. They had backed out of Matt's room and were huddled together in a corner of the kitchen floor.

"I'm scared, Ben," Abby cried. "Matt's really lost it this time. He really *is* crazy."

Ben tried to remain calm. "Abby, it's going to be okay. Mom and Dad know what to do. We have to trust them," Ben consoled her.

Ham forced tears from his eyes. "Look, Matt. I'm crying too, so will you trust us and come out?" Matt nodded and slowly eased out from under his bed. Ali hugged him tightly and continued to cry.

"Why are you still crying, Mom?" Matt asked.

"Because you need help, Matt. Your father and I cannot help you. We need to take you somewhere to get some help," Ali told him.

"Where are we going?" he asked.

"We're taking you to the hospital, Matt. They can help you there," Ham answered.

Matt's eyes widened and his face looked terrified. He shoved past Ali and Ham and ran into the kitchen. He grabbed a large knife out of a drawer.

"I'll kill myself," Matt threatened. "I won't let you take me. I'll kill you if you try to stop me." He didn't see Ben and Abby in the kitchen. Ben slipped silently behind Matt and grabbed the knife as Abby jumped out and startled Matt. Ham and Ali dashed into the kitchen in time to see Ben grab the knife away from Matt.

"Ben's trying to kill me. He's one of them," Matt screamed.

"No he's not, Matt," Ali assured him. "There are no aliens. There never were. It's all in your mind. You've lost touch with reality. We need to go to the hospital right now."

CHAPTER 11
Hospital Food is Great

It was an unusually warm evening for November and the sky was filled with many bright, twinkling stars, but Ali felt very cold and afraid deep inside. Her body shivered so hard that her shell seemed to rattle. Ali called her sister Kate to see if she would watch Ben and Abby while she and Ham took Matt to the hospital. Matt screamed angry insults at his mother the entire trip to the hospital. He continued to threaten to kill them and it almost seemed to please Matt that his mother was so distraught.

Arriving at the children's unit of the University Psychiatric Hospital, Ali wrapped her claws tightly around Matt and carried him inside. He struggled to break free, but Ali's grip was too strong.

"Mom, let go of me. You're hurting me," Matt cried.

"No, I'm not," she retorted. "Be still or you'll hurt yourself."

She stepped up to the check-in desk.

"Hello, my name is Ali Lavar and this is my son Matt," Ali said calmly. "Matt tried to kill himself and his entire family tonight." The receptionist, a small diamond-back turtle, replied, "Sounds like you folks have had a rough evening. Did you call your doctor before you came?"

"No, Ma'am," Ali said. "I felt like it was an emergency."

"Oh," the turtle answered. "How about your insurance company? Did you check with them before coming?"

"Excuse me, Miss, but I have a child who thinks everyone is an alien including you, and he wants to kill them. Do you really think I should wait around for the insurance company to decide if he needs to be in the hospital while he kills himself or someone else? We had to wrestle a knife away from him tonight. I don't believe this could wait, do you?" Ali asked in an annoyed tone.

Ali hadn't noticed that her grip on Matt had relaxed. He had wiggled loose enough to swing himself around and over on top of her shell. Matt quickly had his claw around her neck and was strangling her in front of the receptionist. As Ali made gasping and gurgling sounds, the receptionist quickly pushed a red button on the phone console on her desk and two large lobsters appeared through the automatic double doors.

"Yes, Ma'am?" one asked.

"Help that lady, please," she requested. They forcefully pulled Matt off of Ali, and they continued to restrain him.

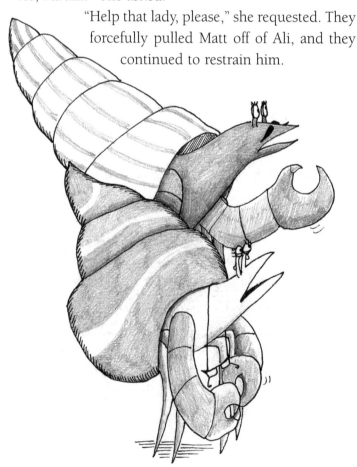

"Let me go," Matt yelled. "I hate you. You're all gonna die."

Ali swallowed hard. "Thank you," she whispered. Ham hurried in through the front doors.

"I couldn't find a parking place…why are they holding Matt like that?" Ham asked. Ali was still rubbing her neck and swallowing.

"Your son just tried to strangle your wife," the turtle informed him. The receptionist didn't really sound upset or surprised. She acted as though it had happened a few times before, and it probably had.

"What?" Ham asked loudly. "Ali, are you okay?" He put his claw around her. She nodded. He got right up in Matt's

face. "As for you, son, I only hope there really is something wrong with you. You're not welcome back in my house until your behavior changes."

"That's okay," Matt said. "I don't want to be there anyway."

The automatic doors opened again and a brown spotted leopard frog with a white nurse's cap hopped out into the waiting area.

"The Lavar family," she called. Ali raised her claw. "Please follow me."

The lobsters released Matt, but one walked on each side of him to the intake area. There they met a child psychiatrist named Dr. Plover. He had short and thin, grayish sandpiper legs, a white chest and chin and dark gray wings and tail. He had a brown spot on his head like a cap and a gray band around his neck like a bow tie. He had a medium black beak and dark brown eyes.

"Hello, I'm Dr. Plover, and I'll be taking care of your son while he is here."

"I'm Ham Lavar. This is my wife Ali, and that's our son Matt," Ham replied.

"It's nice to meet you," Dr. Plover said. He looked over at Matt who was curled up in the corner of the room. Matt turned away.

Dr. Plover turned back to Ali and Ham. "We are usually the last stop on a long and terrible roller coaster ride. I'm sure that the battle has raged for quite a while in your home and in your hearts before you ever considered coming to us. I know you're tired and feel very lonely right now. You're afraid to leave your child here, but you are equally afraid to have him at home. You're at the end of your rope. You've come here because there is no other place to turn," Dr. Plover spoke gently. His words cut deeply into Ali's heart and her tears started to flow once more.

"Finally someone who understands how I feel," she thought. Ham put his claw around her. Matt made spitting noises in the corner of the room.

"From what you've told me, Ms. Lavar, and the records from Dr. Tory," Dr. Plover said, "I believe that Matt is experiencing something called rapid cycling or fast mood swings. This means his moods may move from laughter to tears to anger to depression and back again very quickly. All this can occur in minutes, hours or days. We see this in childhood-onset bipolar disorder. In adult bipolar disorder, the cycles occur more slowly over weeks to months. Matt's brain chemistry is out of balance and we need to find the right medications to help restore that balance. The right medicine will help him think normally again."

"You mean our son wasn't abducted by aliens?" Ham laughed. "What a relief."

A smile suddenly appeared on Ali's face. "You're a nut, Ham," she said gently prodding him.

"No, seriously, you can help my son?" Ham asked.

"Yes, I believe we can, Mr. Lavar," Dr. Plover replied with a smile.

As Ali and Ham tried to hug Matt and say good-bye, he hissed and spit at them.

"I hate you," Matt said.

"That's okay," Ali replied, "because I still love you. I have enough love for both of us." Ham tried to hug Matt, but he pulled away.

"You don't love me. You're leaving me here to die," Matt

said angrily.

"No, son, that's the farthest thing from the truth," Ham assured. A tear slid down the front of Ham's shell. His voice was filled with emotion as he choked out, "We just want you to get well."

As Ali and Ham walked out the double doors, they could hear Matt screaming at them. By then it was close to midnight and physical exhaustion along with the emotional effect of Matt's behavior was taking its toll on them. They felt like ghosts in the crisp night air: empty, weightless and dead.

§

"My head, my head," Matt thought. "It feels like it's going to explode."

The lights seemed so bright and the faces seemed to blur. The voices faded down a long tunnel. The walls were gray and the floor was covered with blue carpet. There were no pictures on the walls. The doors seemed to slam shut behind him, and Matt knew he could not get away. He thrashed around like a wild animal striking out at anyone close to him. He hit a nurse with his claw and then he felt a sharp pain.

"What was that?" he yelled. The lobsters had returned. "But this was different," he thought. "Like a needle."

"Something to calm you down, Matt," Dr. Plover said. "We can't help you until you can control yourself."

"I'm gonna kill you, toooo," Matt's words began to slur as the medication took effect. He slumped down and the lobsters loosened their grip.

"Carry him to his room, please," Dr. Plover requested.

"Hopefully, he will feel better in the morning."

§

"Rise and shine, Matt, it's time for breakfast," the cheerful brown toad called. "I'm Mim, and I'll be looking after you today."

Matt shook his head. It felt heavy. The morning sun was shining through the bare window and onto his bed. Matt noticed there were bars on the window.

"Am I in prison?" he asked. "If not, why are there bars on my window?"

"No, you're not in prison, but the bars are there to keep you from flying off without an airplane," Mim replied with a smile and a wink.

Matt joined four other kids at the breakfast table. The cafeteria was larger than the one at school. The floor had white tile set with different colors to make an interlocking square design. The walls were bright green and decorated with pictures of famous movie stars.

"These pancakes are really good," Matt said. The others nodded. "I'm Matt, so who are you?"

"I'm Tip," the robust brown bullfrog replied. "I set the neighbor's house on fire while they were on vacation."

"Why?" Matt asked.

"Not sure," Tip answered. "Just wanted to see if it would burn."

"I'm Pete and I tried to kill my sister," the young, angry snapping turtle said. "I almost got her too." Matt rolled his eyes in disbelief.

"I'm Will," the only other hermit crab replied. He was

older and larger than Matt with a shell that had endured many battles with other crabs. It had numerous chips and scraped areas. Everyone waited for him to say more.

"That's all, just Will."

All eyes turned to the final member at the table. He was busy stuffing his beak with pancakes and ignoring everyone else. He was a small, young sea gull, and he was eating so fast that they all stopped and stared at him.

"Edgar, what are you doing?" Tip asked. "Last time you ate like that you threw up." Edgar looked up in time to see four pairs of eyes looking at him. He stopped. He gasped and then he gagged suddenly.

"Uh oh," Tip said. "Better duck, he's gonna hurl." Edgar grabbed his beak and headed for the boy's restroom. The boys started laughing.

"What time do we go to the gym?" Will asked.

"There's a gym here?" Matt asked.

"Yeah, it's pretty nice," Will replied. "They got a pool too, but I like to play basketball."

"We gotta go to therapy first," Tip reminded.

"Yuck," Pete said. "I hate to draw, except for hand guns, rifles and bowie knives." Matt flinched.

When Edgar returned to the table, his face was a little pale.

"Are you okay, Edgar?" Tip asked. Edgar nodded and sat down next to Matt. Matt scooted over a little to give him more room just in case he had any more problems with his breakfast.

"Edgar doesn't talk much," Tip said. "They say something really bad happened to him. He cries a lot." Edgar nodded and looked down.

Mim came over to the table. "Breakfast is over. It's time

for your sessions," she said. They carried their trays to the cleanup area and headed up the stairs.

§

Later that evening Matt was able to talk to his mother on the phone.

"Hi, Mom," Matt spoke into the phone on the ward.

"How are you feeling, Matt?" Ali asked carefully. She was holding back her tears. His voice sounded cheerful and not angry. She couldn't see him for two days. A phone call was her only connection.

"Oh, okay I guess," Matt replied.

"What did you do today?" she asked as she searched for the right words.

"We played in the gym. We had pancakes for breakfast and grilled-cheese sandwiches for lunch. The food here is great," Matt said.

"Did you talk to Dr. Plover today?" Ali asked.

"Yeah," Matt replied.

"What did he say, Matt?" she asked.

"Well, he told me I was taking a new medicine to help me feel better. It will help me think right or something like that."

"That sounds good," Ali said. "Have you met any other kids?"

"Yeah," Matt replied. "Um, there's Pete and Will and Tip and…what's that other kid's name? Edgar, I think. He's real quiet. He never talks."

"I miss you," Ali said. It slipped out. She didn't mean to say it.

"I miss you too, Mom," Matt said. "When you gonna come get me?"

Ali swallowed hard. "I can't visit for two more days," she choked out. Tears began to flow down her antennae. "I'm sorry, but that's what Dr. Plover told us."

"Well, okay," Matt said. His voice sounded disappointed. "My time's up, Mom. I gotta go. I'll talk to you tomorrow night. Bye."

"Goodnight, sweetheart," Ali sobbed quietly. "I love you very much."

And Matt was gone. Ali continued to cry until she could barely breathe.

"Please don't cry, Momma," a little voice said behind her. She turned to find Abby. "Don't you love us?"

"Of course I do, Abby, but my heart is broken because Matt is sick and I miss him very much," Ali explained. Abby climbed up in her lap and hugged her.

"I love you, Momma," Abby said. Ali hugged her back.

"I love you too, Abby," Ali said. "Thanks for the hug. I needed it."

§

Later that night, Matt was lying in his bed trying to sleep. "What's all that noise?" Matt wondered. The loud voices and occasional curse word caught his attention. He hurried over to the window. He looked out into the courtyard to see adults smoking and talking very loudly. It was way past his bedtime. "How can I sleep with all that noise?" he thought. Then he noticed that there were no hospital staff with them. He hurried to find a nurse to tell.

"There's people outside my window talking very loud," Matt reported.

"There are?" Winston, the night nurse, said. "Show me where." Matt took the nurse into his room and pointed out the noisy crew below his window. "They're not supposed to be outside this time of night. Thanks, Matt, for telling me. Now go back to bed and I'll take care of it." In a few minutes, Matt heard Winston's voice outside telling everyone to come in. He was not happy that they had disturbed his young patients above them, and they were no longer allowed outside after 9 PM. Matt could hear their angry voices and cursing at Winston for making them leave. Matt sat on his bed and giggled about causing such trouble for grownups.

§

Ali and Ham were nervous as they walked through the double doors into the locked children's psychiatric unit. They had not been allowed in this part of the hospital when Matt was admitted.

"It looks like a hospital," Ali thought. Everyone had a private room although there were two beds in some of the rooms. Matt's room was at the end of the hall. He was in the TV room when they arrived.

"Look who's here to see you, Matt," Mim announced. Matt looked up from the football game.

"Hi, Mom," he said and gave her a hug. "Hi, Dad." He gave him a high clap in the air with his claw.

"How are you feeling, Matt?" Ali asked.

"Doin' okay," he said.

"Where's your room?" Ham asked.

"Oh, it's down the hall. Come on, I'll show you," Matt said as he headed out of the room. Ali and Ham followed. "Well, here it is. Not much to see. Just my bed, my bathroom and a place for my clothes. And here's where I got those guys in trouble for waking me up one night." Matt started giggling. Ali looked out the window into the small courtyard below.

"Do you ever get to go outside?" she asked.

"No, we're too high risk for flight," Matt replied. "That means we might run away." Ali nodded.

"What do you do during the day?" Ham asked.

"We go to the gym two or three times if we're good. If not, we don't. We go to sessions and talk and draw stuff. We go to the cafeteria and the food is great. We see a movie if we're good. That kind of stuff," Matt answered.

"Sounds like they keep you pretty busy," Ali said.

"Yeah and we have to take pills too," Matt added. The trio had moved back down the hall to the TV room again and Tip was now busy building a model airplane. They sat down in one corner of the room.

"So when do I get to go home?" Matt asked.

"I don't know," Ali answered.

"I'm trying to be good. I get to go home sooner if I'm good," Matt volunteered.

Ham couldn't resist the temptation. "Matt, do you still believe that aliens have taken over the earth?" he asked. Ali frowned and gave Ham a hard nudge. Matt stared at him oddly.

"Dad, are you nuts?" Matt replied. "Of course not." Ham looked relieved. Mim appeared at the door. She was looking down at her watch.

"I think it's time for you to go," Matt said sadly. Ali had to fight back the tears again.

"Give me a hug," Ali said. "I love you, Matt." He hugged her tightly and also hugged his dad.

"Bye, Mom. Bye, Dad. I love you too," Matt said.

"The next time we come, it will be to take you home," Ali uttered softly as tears welled up in her eyes.

"Please don't cry, Mom," Matt begged. "I don't want to see you cry because of me."

"You'll be home soon and then I'll be happy again," she answered. Matt nodded and smiled.

CHAPTER 12
Home for the Holidays

Tears of joy filled Ali's eyes when Dr. Plover called to say that she could come take Matt home that afternoon. It was the day before Thanksgiving. As she stepped outside into the morning sunshine, Ali felt the cool breeze and watched as the young crabs laughed and played on the seashore.

"Good morning, Ali," one of the neighboring sea gulls called as she flew overhead.

"Good morning, Sue," Ali replied. "Matt's coming home today."

"That's wonderful," Sue answered and waved as she flew away. Ali felt very happy.

"I need to tell the family and Matt's teacher," Ali said quietly to herself. "I wonder what Ms. Kay has told the class about his absence?"

Abby and Ben were at school and Ham had already left for work. Ali was pacing around the yard trying to decide what to do next. She must have looked funny because she was startled by the stares and laughter of three little girl crabs giggling at her. She looked over at them.

"Oh my, who are you?" she inquired. The trio continued to giggle. "Am I that funny looking?" They all nodded and held their claws up to their faces.

"Where's your mother? Won't she be looking for you?" Ali asked.

"She's over dare," one of the little girls replied and pointed.

"Well you need to get back to her or she will worry. Run

along now," Ali shooed them down the beach toward their mother. The little girl crabs continued to giggle the entire way. It made Ali smile and chuckle. It felt so good to laugh again. Ali went back in the house and sat down on the couch. She picked up the book she had been reading since Matt was admitted to the hospital. She was almost finished with the book *The Bipolar Crab*. It had explained so many things about Matt's behavior.

"I only wish I had read this before Matt went into the hospital," Ali thought. "I wonder if Ms. Kay might want to read this when I'm finished?"

The phone rang. She hurried to answer it.

"Hello," she said.

"This is Ham. Did you need me for something?" he asked.

"Oh, hi honey," Ali answered, "I just wanted to let you know that Dr. Plover is releasing Matt from the hospital today."

"What time?" he asked.

"I'm supposed to go get him after four o' clock," she replied.

"That's great news," Ham said.

"Yes, I'm so happy," Ali agreed.

"I'll see you tonight then. The whole family that is," Ham emphasized and smiled to himself.

"We'll be here. Maybe we can go out to eat to celebrate. Oh, I forgot tomorrow is Thanksgiving. Well, we definitely have something to be thankful for," Ali replied. "We'll do something special for Thanksgiving Day."

"Sounds good to me," Ham said. "See you later."

Ali decided to clean up Matt's room and decorate it for

his homecoming. She pushed open the door and moved aside the items stacked up in piles. She had refused to go in since he had been hospitalized. She cried every time she looked in Matt's room. Now he was coming home and she could face the task of cleaning it. She was shocked to find that several of his prized soccer trophies were broken. A signed poster of one of his favorite stars was ripped up. Ali found notebook paper with almost unreadable handwriting that spoke of aliens taking over and how he was the last survivor. It described in gruesome detail how to kill the aliens.

Ali was so horrified that she wadded up the papers and threw them into the garbage. She found the broken pieces of the trophies and glued them back together. She carefully taped back together the signed poster as best she could and mounted it back on Matt's wall. When she finished, his room was clean and it appeared much like it did before his moods started changing so much. She added one final touch: a "Welcome Home" banner that she made by herself.

§

Matt was all smiles as he said his good-byes to the hospital staff. Ali carried Matt's little suitcase and held him close as they walked outside. Abby and Ben were waiting in the car.

"Do you think he's okay now?" Abby asked.

Ben thought for a moment and replied, "Well Abby, the doctors are letting him come home so he must be pretty much okay. I don't think they'd let him out if he was still acting crazy." Abby nodded. Matt climbed into the front seat and buckled his seatbelt. He turned around and looked at Abby and Ben.

"Did you miss me?" he asked.

"The house was deadly quiet without you," Ben replied with a grin.

Abby turned her head away and said, "I liked the peace and quiet."

"At least I got one vote," Matt replied.

"Let's go home," Ali said and started the engine.

Matt went to his room and saw what Ali had done.

"Mom," Matt called, "thanks for the welcome home sign. You fixed my trophies too."

Ali came into his room. She looked around and smiled.

"Do you like it?" she asked.

"Sure," Matt answered and gave her a hug. "What's for dinner?"

"How about bean burritos?" Ali offered.

"Sounds great," Matt replied. "Any dessert?"

"Does cake sound good?" she asked.

"You bet," he answered. "You're a wonderful mom."

"I'm glad we agree on that one," she laughed.

Ali noticed that Matt ate a lot more food than usual, especially dessert. The next morning she was shocked to find that her kitchen floor was littered with candy wrappers.

"Abby, Ben, Matt," Ali called. "Who ate all these candy bars last night?"

All three came into the kitchen to see what she was talking about.

"Good grief," Abby said. "Somebody's got a sweet tooth."

"Looks like someone has a whole mouthful," Ben chuckled. Matt said nothing.

"Matt," Ali said, "you're awfully quiet. Don't you have an opinion about our mysterious midnight snacker?"

"No," Matt replied.

"Because it's you," Abby accused.

"So what!" Matt said getting defensive. Ali saw a fight coming on and quickly moved to stop it.

"That's okay, Matt," Ali said. "Just let me know next time and I'll try to have healthier snacks for you to eat. And please clean up after yourself. You do it at school, so please do it at home also."

"I get hungry, Mom," Matt whined. "My stomach wakes me up at night. I can't help it."

"Don't worry, Matt," she reassured. "Dr. Plover warned

me that you might eat more while taking this medicine. I just didn't think about you being hungry after all the dinner you ate. We'll plan ahead tonight so you won't feel so desperate." Matt nodded. Ali gave him a hug.

Abby turned to Ben and whispered, "So Matt's turned into a pig now." Ben shook his head and tried to quiet her giggling.

"Abby," Ali said. "How would you like it if someone said that about you?" Abby turned around and blushed.

"I guess…," she replied. "I wouldn't like it."

"Then don't say it," Ali insisted. "Your brother has been through a lot this past week and he doesn't need your insults. Please be more considerate of his feelings."

"Yes, Ma'am," Abby said dropping her head in shame.

For Thanksgiving Dinner they joined Ali's father and her sister's family to celebrate at a local restaurant. Ali noticed that Matt seemed more nervous with extra crabs around. While she was talking to her sister, Matt repeatedly interrupted her conversation.

"What is it now, Matt?" Ali asked, annoyed by his interruptions.

"I need to go to the restroom," Matt said.

"You know where it is, dear," Ali said. "Help yourself." Matt jumped up and ran to the restroom as fast as he could go.

"That's odd," Ham noticed. "Is Matt okay? He ran like he had an emergency."

"I don't know, Ham," Ali replied. "He's gone to the men's room and I can't follow, so why don't you go check on him?" Ham nodded and left to find Matt.

"Is everything okay?" her sister Kate asked.

"I think so," Ali replied. "Matt has been doing a few weird things, but I think it's the medicine he's taking that's causing the problem."

"Oh," Kate said and started eating her dinner again.

"Well, have they figured out what made Matt go crazy that night, Ali?" her father asked.

"Yeah, Dad," Ali replied. "Matt has bipolar disorder."

"What's that?" he asked.

"It's another name for manic depression. Matt has a chemical imbalance in his brain that makes him have mood swings and rage attacks. But the medicine seems to be helping him so far," Ali answered.

"Where'd he get it? I don't know anybody with that?" her dad asked.

"Well, it seems to be inherited, but it may have come through Ham's family, not ours. There are a lot of people with this disorder who have not been properly diagnosed and remain untreated. So it could be in our family, but we don't recognize it," she replied.

"So are you saying one of us is crazy too?" Kate asked.

"No," Ali declared. "I didn't say that. Having bipolar disorder doesn't mean you're crazy. Some famous and very talented crabs, turtles, frogs and sea gulls were bipolar. Sir Phig Newton, the mathematician, and Baywoven, the composer, had classic symptoms starting in childhood. Some of our greatest leaders and writers like Honest Lincoln, Winsome Churchill, Samuel Twain and Edgar Raven had symptoms that today would be diagnosed as bipolar. Some of our famous actors and writers have stepped forward to help us understand the disorder better by sharing their lives with us. Matt has it and it doesn't matter where it came from. We just have to make sure he stays on the medicine."

"Oh," Kate said.

"Besides," Ali continued, "it's nobody's fault. You can't blame anyone for what you inherit. And blaming doesn't do any good. It doesn't help anybody and especially Matt. He can't help it that he has this problem. Blaming him will only upset him even more."

Ham returned with Matt from the restroom.

"Are you okay?" Ali asked. Matt shook his head.

"He got nervous and made himself sick," Ham related quietly. "We took care of it and he seems a little better now."

Ali gave Matt a hug. "I'm sorry," she whispered. "Do you want anything else to eat or do you just want to go home?"

Matt looked up into his mother's eyes and said, "I don't want to mess up Thanksgiving for you, Mom. But I'm not hungry anymore."

"Can we finish our dinner or do we need to leave now?" she asked.

"I want to go home," Matt replied. Ali quickly explained to her sister and father that Matt's stomach was upset and that she needed to take him home. Her father offered to bring the rest of the family home when they finished their dinner.

"What's wrong with Matt?" Abby asked. "Did he throw up or something?"

"Yes, he did," Ali replied.

"Ooh, yuck," Abby said. "How gross, Matt."

"That's enough, Abby," Ham ordered sharply. Ali bundled Matt up and helped him out to the car.

"It could be the medicine making you sick," Ali suggested. "I'll get you home so you can lie down."

"Thanks, Mom," Matt replied weakly. Ali was disappointed. She wanted Thanksgiving Day to be perfect for Matt and the family, but it hadn't turned out that way.

"At least I have my family back together again," she thought. "They aren't perfect, but they're all I've got." She sighed and drove Matt home.

CHAPTER 13
Back to School with a New Attitude

Matt recovered from his Thanksgiving Day sickness. On Friday morning Ali wanted to go to the mall. The family decided to take a vote for shopping or a movie. The movie won easily 4 to 1.

"But I want to go shopping," Ali said with a childish whine. "Well, I get to pick the movie then." It made everyone laugh. Ali smiled. Her family was happy again. Matt still had a couple of times when he got upset that weekend, but he was so much better that no one complained, not even Abby.

Early Monday morning Ali awoke suddenly. Matt was sleeping on the floor again just like old times.

"Matt," she whispered loudly, "are you okay?" He was sound asleep and she decided not to wake him up. However she did wake up Ham accidentally.

"I'm a little nervous," Ali confided.

"About what?" Ham asked.

"Matt going back to school today," she replied.

"Why?" he asked and yawned sleepily.

"I don't know. I guess because I'm not sure how the kids at school will react to Matt. I don't know what Ms. Kay has told them about him being in the hospital," Ali related.

"Well, if you don't know, I wouldn't worry about it. Ms. Kay seems to be a good teacher. I would go talk to her. Take your book and ask her if she would like to read about Matt's condition."

"That's a good idea, dear," Ali replied. "I just finished it yesterday. I'll take Matt in early and see if I can talk to her this morning before school starts. Thanks, honey. Honey?" She rolled over to find that Ham had fallen back to sleep. Ali yawned and fell back to sleep also.

The alarm buzzed loudly and Ali swatted at it to make the awful noise stop.

"It couldn't be time to get up," she thought. "I just went to bed." She rolled over and pushed herself out of bed. "Ben, Matt, Abby," she called half-heartedly. "Time to get up."

"We're already up, Mom," Abby replied.

"Oh good," Ali mumbled. "I'm so tired. Coffee, gotta get some coffee." She shuffled to the kitchen and heated up day-old coffee. Ben, Matt, and Abby were busy eating their breakfast. Ben was having cereal and milk. He had made Abby and Matt toast topped with butter, cinnamon and sugar. They all appeared to be very content.

"Mom," Matt asked. "My friends will still remember me, won't they?"

"I'm sure they will," Ali replied. "That's what I'm afraid of."

"What do you mean?" Matt asked with a puzzled look on his face.

"Well," Ali replied, regretting having made the comment. "Their last encounter with you was not pleasant."

"Oh," he said. "I see what you mean. Do you think you could tell them I'm okay now?"

"I don't know what to say," Ali admitted. "I plan to talk to Ms. Kay this morning. I think she knows that you're coming back today. Be nice to everyone and win their trust back. That's all I know to tell you." Matt nodded. "Let's get going. We need to leave soon."

Ali headed down the hall to Ms. Kay's room with the book *The Bipolar Crab* in her front claw. News had traveled of Matt's hospitalization and a couple of teachers asked how Matt was doing. Ali assured them that he was much better.

"How are you this morning?" Ali asked as she stood in the door. Ms. Kay looked up and smiled.

"Come in, Ms. Lavar," Ms. Kay said. "Tell me, is Matt coming back today?"

"Yes, Ma'am, he is," Ali said. "I brought you this book. It's all about his bipolar disorder. It's very good and has helped me understand him so much better. I only wish I had read it months ago when I started noticing gradual changes in his mood. It would've saved us a lot of heartache."

"Thank you so much," Ms. Kay replied thoughtfully. "I welcome and appreciate any resource that helps me learn and understand more about the needs of my students. Matt has definitely kept me busy trying to learn more this year."

"I'm sorry that he's been such a handful. I know he has been a lot of trouble for you," Ali apologized.

"No," Ms. Kay replied. "He has reminded me why I went into teaching in the first place. I wanted to help students like Matt who have special needs. I want to be that special kind of teacher who can help them."

"Thank you for understanding and caring about Matt," Ali said with a smile. "He seems to be much better. I see the old Matt returning. He smiles more and laughs and even hugs me like he used to." A tear rolled down the front of her shell and then another. Ms. Kay offered a tissue and Ali nodded.

"Matt will do fine," Ms. Kay reassured and patted Ali's shell with her wing. At this point a stream of various young

crabs, lobsters, turtles, frogs, sea gulls, and sandpipers rushed around Ali as she stood just inside the doorway.

"I'd better be going," Ali said. Matt came by and gave her a hug.

"Did you tell her, Mom?" he asked.

"Yes, I did. I'll see you at home this afternoon," Ali replied and hugged him back.

Matt's first day back went fairly smoothly. He got a little frustrated at lunch trying to open a milk carton. He also had difficulty copying his spelling words because his claws were shaking when he tried to write. Ms. Kay took note of these things and worked to keep the environment as calm as possible around Matt. The other students were still distant and a little fearful of Matt. He sensed this anxiety in his classmates and it made him sad.

§

After a week or so, Ms. Kay had read enough of *The Bipolar Crab* to start following some of the suggestions for teachers. She arranged to have Matt use a small computer on his desk instead of having to write everything. This helped him so much and his grades improved. Ms. Kay also established a safe and quiet place for Matt to go when he felt like he was losing control. He could go out in the hall to his special place and relax. He was allowed to get water and go to the restroom whenever he needed because of the medications he was taking. She encouraged him to tell her when he felt frustrated or upset so she could try to help him. However, Ms. Kay noticed her class was still somewhat afraid of him. They feared that he would erupt into the violent, angry Matt who had gone into the hospital. Ms. Kay decided to help the class understand his condition.

"Matt," Ms. Kay asked. "Would you mind if I told the class about your bipolar disorder?"

Matt looked surprised. "No, Ma'am," he said. "That would be okay."

"I think it would help everyone if they knew more about it, don't you?" she asked. Matt nodded. That morning instead of reading time, Ms. Kay gathered the class into a circle on the reading carpet. Matt sat next to her.

"Class," she said. "I want to tell you about someone very special in your group. His name is Matt." Some of the girls giggled and a few boys were punching each other. "Matt had to spend a week in the hospital recently and we all made cards for him. I never told you why he went to the hospital. Matt suffers from something called bipolar disorder. His brain gets out of balance and causes his moods to change quickly and many times he cannot control them. He may get angry and yell at you, but not really feel that way about you. But because he has this problem, he does things that are exaggerated beyond his normal feelings. It makes him very sensitive to what you say or do, so you need to think before you say things that might upset him. He is still the funny and nice crab we all once knew, but this disorder hides the real Matt sometimes. When he gets upset, stay calm and don't try to reason with him until he has calmed down. Do you have any questions?"

Todd raised his claw. "Ms. Kay, is this bipolar contagious?" he asked.

More giggles rippled through the classroom. Matt even giggled.

"No, Todd," Matt answered. "I was born with it so you can't catch it from me." Todd looked relieved.

Billy raised a claw. "Matt," he asked. "Do you have to take medicine for it?" Matt nodded.

"Yes, I do," Matt said, "but it's not too bad. It has helped me control my thinking better and I don't feel as angry and sad like I used to. It makes my claws shake and that's why I have to use the computer to write."

Julie, a small sandpiper, raised her wing. "Ms. Kay, is there anything we can do to help?" she asked. Ms. Kay's face lit up with a smile.

"Julie, I'm so glad you asked that question," Ms. Kay said. "In fact, there is something you can do. You can help me keep an eye on Matt and if you see that he is getting upset and I'm not watching or I'm not in the room, please come get me and help Matt to his quiet place." Julie and the class all nodded.

After that day, Matt's classmates were no longer afraid of him and they tried to help him whenever they could.

§

Ingo, the flamingo, had just moved into the area. He didn't know anyone, and he was afraid to go to school. Ms. Rolle brought Ingo to Ms. Kay's room.

"Ingo, this is Ms. Kay and this is her class," Ms. Rolle said.

"Hello, Ingo," Ms. Kay said. "Have you moved here recently?" Ingo nodded shyly. "We'll get you some books and a desk with your name on it. Sit here next to Matt." Ingo sat down beside Matt's desk.

"Hi, I'm Matt," Matt said. "Your name is Ingo? Is that right?" Ingo nodded. "Where are you from?"

"Mexico," he replied.

"Wow, I've never met anyone from Mexico. That's so neat," Matt said.

"Really?" Ingo answered. "You like I am from Mexico?"

"Yeah, that's cool. You must speak Spanish too?" Matt asked.

"Si, amigo," Ingo replied. Matt smiled and Ingo smiled too. Matt helped Ingo get his books, his locker, his lunch and his assignments. He helped Ingo get adjusted to his new school and made him feel welcome. Ingo taught Matt some Spanish words.

§

A couple of weeks later, Todd's father, a professional songwriter, offered to come and help the class write a song.

They were all very excited. He brought his guitar to accompany the class.

"So what do you want the title of the song to be?" Todd's dad asked. Many suggestions filled the air and the noise was deafening.

"Okay, okay class," Ms. Kay called. "Raise your claw, leg or wing and speak one at a time."

"How about *A Nebula Bar*?" Matt suggested. The class all agreed that this would be a fun title.

"Now we need lyrics," Todd's dad said.

"It's chewy and chocolate," Julie said.

"And caramel," Billy added.

"That makes me hungry," Matt replied.

"I wanna yell for a Nebula bar," Joey yelled.

"Stop now," Todd's father said. "Let's put this together. I think we have something." He started to strum on his guitar and sing.

"I want a Nebula bar, give me a Nebula bar. A yummy Nebula bar, oh please…give me a Nebula bar.

Chewy chocolate caramel makes me hungry, I wanna yell for a Nebula bar."

"Okay," he said. "Let's do one more verse. What else can you think of about Nebula bars?"

"Well, they're not nutritious," Carl offered.

"But they're delicious," Sue, a small green turtle, called out.

"Feels so yummy in my tummy," Matt added.

"Let me write this down. Okay now. Let's put it all together," Todd's dad instructed. "Join me when you're ready."

"I want a Nebula bar, give me a Nebula bar;
A yummy Nebula bar, oh please… give me a Nebula bar.

Chewy chocolate caramel, makes me hungry;
I wanna yell for a Nebula bar.

Not nutritious, but delicious;
Feels so yummy in my tummy.

I want a Nebula bar, give me a Nebula bar;
A yummy Nebula bar, oh please… give me a Nebula bar."

The class all laughed and sang loudly with Todd's father. A week later Todd brought each classmate a compact disk with the song recorded on it. Matt was so excited to share it with his family. They all sat around listening and laughing.

"So who wrote the words?" Ben asked.

"We did. My class did," Matt said.

"Who was that crab singing and playing the guitar?" Abby asked.

"That's Todd's dad," Matt replied. "He's a songwriter."

"It sounded very…tasteful for a crab's Nebula bar," Ali said.

"Oh, Mom," the three groaned and laughed.

CHAPTER 14
The Final Weeks

"Where's my bag of balloons?" Matt called as he raced around the kitchen searching for it.

"What balloons are you talking about?" Ali asked as Matt brushed by.

"The ones I have to take to school," he said. "You know, Mom, for field day today."

"Oh, those balloons," she replied. "They're in your backpack. Didn't you look there first?"

"No, I didn't," Matt admitted. He stopped and pulled open the backpack and checked to make sure his mother was correct. He held them up and counted them.

"Be sure and put them back," Ali said. "Have you eaten breakfast yet?"

"Yeah, I had some cereal and a doughnut," Matt replied.

"Ben, Abby, have you had breakfast?" Ali called. Muffled replies echoed down the hall. "Was that a yes or no?" Ben and Abby came out of their rooms.

"Mom, I told you I had breakfast," Abby answered a little irritated. Ben giggled at Abby when he saw her hiding a tube of lipstick behind her back. "What are you laughing at?" she demanded.

"You have Mom's lipstick on the back of your shell," he snickered. She was outraged and quickly ran into the bathroom to clean it off.

"What did you say, Ben?" Ali asked. "Abby has my lipstick...on the back of her shell?" Ben was still laughing at Abby who was furiously scrubbing the back of her shell.

She was not happy about being caught with Mom's make-up without permission. Ali came down the hall to find out why Abby was suddenly so interested in cleaning up. When she saw the lipstick mark on the back of Abby's shell, she had to turn away to hide her amusement.

"I'll help you, Abby," Ali said with a slight giggle. She reached to clean off the red mark high on the back of Abby's shell. "You weren't trying to hide anything from me, were you?"

"Uh, no, well, yes, Ma'am," Abby stuttered. "I took your lipstick. I just wanted to see how it would look on me." Ali nodded.

"Please ask next time," Ali requested.

"Yes, Ma'am," Abby said.

"Well, it's time to go to school," Ali said. Everyone headed out the door.

Matt hurried into his classroom and took out the bag of balloons.

"Look, Ms. Kay," he said. "I brought twenty balloons. What are we going to do with them?"

"You'll see very soon, Matt," Ms. Kay answered with a big smile. Field day was always special because the parents got involved. The kids spent most of the day outside doing wacky relays and other fun events and enjoyed ice cream and cold treats at the end of the crazy competitions. As the class rushed outside, Matt could feel his heart pounding. Soon the helper moms appeared with a bucket of water-filled balloons.

"Those are my balloons," Matt said. "Oh, wow, water balloons. This is gonna be so much fun." The moms picked partners and then explained that they were to throw the balloons gently and their partner would try to catch them without breaking them.

They were lined up in two lines facing each other. Matt was paired with Billy. Matt threw first and Billy caught it. Then Billy tossed the orange balloon a little too high and Matt jumped up to catch it. The balloon broke right in his face and knocked him to the ground. He fell hard scraping his leg on a rock. His face was wet and his leg was bleeding. Billy couldn't help it. He started to giggle. He didn't mean to laugh at Matt, but he tended to giggle easily.

"Don't laugh at me," Matt cried as the anger began to build. Billy tried to suppress his laughter. "I said don't laugh at me," Matt yelled. He was up on his feet and heading for Billy like a linebacker after a quarterback. As Matt charged across the field, Billy froze. Matt slammed him down hard.

"Don't hurt me," Billy whimpered. Matt got up. His anger was waning. The helper moms were in a panic by now and had rushed to get Ms. Kay. Billy got up and brushed himself off.

"Are you okay?" Ms. Kay asked Billy. He nodded. "Matt, your leg is bleeding. We need to get you to the clinic and put a bandage on your scrape," Ms. Kay said.

"Yes, Ma'am," Matt replied and followed her to the building. Matt sat silently on the clinic cot while the helper mom told Ms. Kay what happened.

"Billy threw the balloon and then when it broke, Matt got angry and charged him like a bull. He knocked him down. Did he take his medicine today? I thought he was on medication now for his mental disorder," the helper mom questioned.

"Billy laughed at me. That's what made me angry, Ms.

Kay. That balloon hit my face and broke and knocked me down. I scraped my leg and he was laughing," Matt spoke softly. "But I know that what I did was wrong and I'm sorry. Can I tell Billy that I'm sorry, Ms. Kay?"

Ms. Kay looked at the helper mom and said, "See, he did take his medicine. Without medication, he would never have had the ability to see that his actions were not acceptable or what he should do to make up for his inappropriate behavior. He is so much better now." She turned back to Matt.

"Your scrape is all bandaged now. Let's go find Billy and talk this over." Matt and Ms. Kay headed off down the hall together. The helper mom just stood in the clinic with her mouth open in amazement.

"Billy," Ms. Kay said. "Matt has something he would like to say to you."

"Um, I'm sorry about knocking you down outside," Matt said. "I thought you were laughing at me and it made me angry."

"I wasn't laughing at you, Matt," Billy said. "I got to giggling and couldn't stop. I'm sorry I hurt your feelings."

"I hope I didn't hurt you. I didn't mean to, really. I just wanted you to stop laughing," Matt said with his eyes looking down.

"How did you feel, Billy?" Ms. Kay asked.

"Kinda mad," Billy answered.

"No, when you saw Matt charging at you," Ms. Kay said.

"Oh, I was scared," Billy said.

"Do you forgive me?" Matt asked.

"Oh, Matt," Billy replied and put his claw over Matt's shell. "You're still my buddy." Matt and Billy smiled at each other. Ms. Kay had to fight back the tears.

§

A few days later, Matt was sitting at his desk. He was a little frustrated with his class assignment.

"Matt, I've been over this twice. I think you understand what I'm asking you to do. Don't you?" Ms. Kay asked. Matt shook his head and walked over to the door.

"I'm frustrated, Ms. Kay," Matt said. "I need to go to my quiet place." Ms. Kay nodded and Matt slipped out into the hall. He paced out in the hall for a few minutes and giggled. Ms. Kay came out to check on him.

"Matt," she asked. "Are you okay?"

"Yes, Ma'am," he said giggling.

"Are you feeling restless?" she asked. Matt nodded. "Do I need to call your mother?"

"No, Ma'am, I'll be okay," Matt replied. A few minutes later Matt was sitting at his desk pretending to cry. Todd came to tell Ms. Kay.

"Ms. Kay, Matt is crying. He needs help," Todd said. Ms. Kay watched Matt carefully.

"Listen to him," she said. Matt would cry for a minute or two and then would stop and peek out to see if anybody was watching. Then he would start again. "I don't think Matt is really that upset. I think he just wants some attention," Ms. Kay said.

"Oh," Todd said. "How can you tell if he really needs help?"

"Look at his face," she instructed. "When he's in trouble, his face looks very upset and either angry or sad. Right now he looks like he wants...extra homework," she said the last part a little louder so Matt would hear.

"I do not," Matt insisted and dropped his claws away from

his face. He realized that Ms. Kay wasn't fooled by his act. He started to laugh and Todd and Ms. Kay laughed with him.

§

One morning several weeks later, someone brought Ms. Kay a cupcake with chocolate icing. Matt's desk was next to Ms. Kay's so he spotted the delicious dessert right away. She was busy grading papers, and Matt was eyeing the cupcake hungrily.

"Umm, that looks so good, Ms. Kay," Matt said as he tried to steal a taste.

"That's my cupcake, Matt," Ms. Kay sternly, but playfully reminded.

"Can't I just have a little taste?" he asked.

"No, it wouldn't be fair to the class if I gave you a taste and no one else," she explained.

"But I've been so good. I deserve a treat," Matt insisted.

"I'm sorry, but the cupcake was given to me," Ms. Kay replied.

"Well, you look like you've had more than a few cupcakes in your thirty years of teaching, Ms. Kay," Matt teased. Ms. Kay looked up at him.

"Are you sure you're not an alien, Matt?" she asked.

"No, Ms. Kay," Matt replied. "If I were an alien, I would've eaten that cupcake and disappeared by now." He clicked his claw and pretended to disappear. They both laughed.

§

The last day of school arrived and Matt was filled with excitement and sadness. He was excited because tomorrow was the beginning of summer vacation, but he was sad because he would miss his teacher and friends at school.

"Mom, what did you get for Ms. Kay?" Matt called.

"What do you mean what did I get for Ms. Kay?" Ali asked.

"You know, a teacher's gift," he said holding his claws out.

"Well, they were fresh out of sainthood certificates or I would've gotten her one. She has definitely earned one," Ali said thinking with her claw raised to her face.

"Mom," Matt whined quite irritably. "You know what I mean."

"Matt, I got her something very nice. Ms. Kay has been an exceptional teacher and we have been so blessed to have known her at such a critical time in your life. I'm afraid that other teachers would have only seen you as a problem crab instead of a crab with a problem."

"I wonder how many students slip through the system and grow up angry and bitter, so misunderstood by every-one around them," Ali pondered. "Or even worse, never grow up at all."

"Mom, it's time to go to school. Ben and Abby are waiting in the car," Matt reported. Ali and Matt hurried to the car.

School was abuzz with activity as cupcakes and goodies were being carried in by parents. Little crabs, lobsters, sea gulls, sandpipers, turtles, and frogs all scurried about preparing for the last day. Along with the parties, achieve-ment awards would be given out today.

"You know that I will miss you all very much this sum-mer," Ms. Kay said. "This class has meant more to me than any I have taught in the last thirty years. I have learned that one can never stop learning, especially teachers; I've learned

that we must seek to understand and care for those who are different than we are. I am so pleased to see that you as a class have learned this same wonderful lesson. You have shown love and concern for others who don't think like you, talk like you or act like you think they should, and that is a grown-up thing to do. You have learned far more than just math, science and social studies this year."

"I'd like to present the achievement awards for this year." Everyone in the class sat up and wiped the cupcake crumbs from their faces. The desks had all been cleaned out and moved over into one corner, and all the kids sat on the reading rug as Ms. Kay announced the winners.

"For outstanding scholastic achievement, Carmen," Ms. Kay announced. The kids clapped as Carmen, the lobster, came up to accept her certificate.

"For outstanding compassion and caring, Todd," Ms. Kay continued. Todd grinned and took his certificate.

"For an outstanding sense of humor, Billy," she said. Billy giggled and hid his face behind the certificate.

"For outstanding courage, Matt. He not only accepted his disability, but he was willing to teach others about it as well," Ms. Kay said with tears in her eyes. The entire class stood and clapped as Matt walked up to accept his certificate. He grinned and bowed playfully and hurried to sit down.

After all the awards were given out, the parents started arriving to pick up their kids. Each student embraced Ms. Kay and told her how much they would miss her. Finally Ali arrived to pick up Matt.

"Are you ready to go?" Ali asked. "Or has Ms. Kay agreed to take you home for the summer?"

"What?" Ms. Kay said overhearing the conversation.

"Mom, stop teasing," Matt said.

"Who's teasing? Didn't you ask her?" Ali asked with a wink.

"Well, I could use someone to help me clean and fix up the place," Ms. Kay admitted.

"Mom," Matt protested a little louder. "It's time to go home."

"Kids," Ali laughed. "They just can't take a joke."

"Who's joking? You mean he isn't going to paint my cabinets and clean up my attic?" Ms. Kay asked.

"Mom," he said. "We need to go." Matt was getting embarrassed.

"I'm sorry, Ms. Kay, but Matt will have to paint my cabinets and clean my attic first," Ali replied. Matt was stomping around the classroom.

"Oh, well," Ms. Kay lamented, "maybe next year." Ali and Ms. Kay chuckled, and Matt looked annoyed.

"Let's go, Mom. It's time for summer vacation," Matt declared.

"Thank you so much for all that you have done for Matt this year," Ali said. "I know that his journey could've turned out so differently without a caring teacher."

"Matt has shown me how much I still need to learn about kids with chemical imbalances and behavior disorders. I'm getting certified to teach students with these learning disabilities. It has been a good experience for me as well. I'll miss Matt and his unique sense of humor. He has definitely been the spice in my life this year. I hope you all have fun this summer," Ms. Kay said.

"We will," Ali said. They found Ben and Abby waiting outside in front of the school. As they were driving home, Matt looked up suddenly.

"So, what *are* we going to do this summer?" he asked.

"I'm not too worried. I'm sure you'll think of something Matt," Ali replied with a grin. Everyone laughed.

About the Author

Dr. Caroline C. McGee is a board-certified Family Physician who lives near Nashville, Tennessee with her husband and three sons.

She received her medical degree from the University of Tennessee Center for the Health Sciences in Memphis. Dr. McGee completed her residency in Roanoke, Virginia.

She has practiced family medicine for sixteen years and has cared for patients with depression and bipolar disorder. She also works with a Juvenile Detention Center caring for behaviorally troubled youths.

Dr. McGee is a founding board member of Tennessee Women in Medicine, a member of the American Academy of Family Physicians and the Tennessee Academy of Family Physicians. She is also on the board of Siloam Family Health Center, a local indigent clinic, where she serves as a volunteer physician.

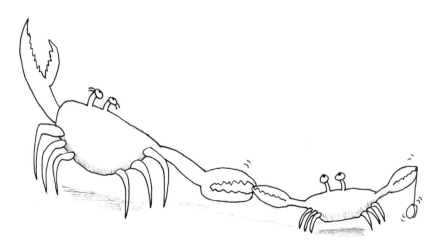